Wishing For Someday Soon

By Tiffany King

www.authortiffanyjking.blogspot.com

To my amazing family, who support me unconditionally. And to my friends and fellow authors, I am inspired by each and every one of you. Finally, to my wonderful editor, Hollie Westring, thank you for all your help with the book.

Chapter 1

When I was younger, I always thought of life like chapters in a book. I never knew what each turn of the page would bring, but always hoped for something better and happier. I regarded my younger brother and myself as characters that were meant to persevere, no matter what obstacles were thrown our way. Of course, our life was far from the paranormal worlds that I loved reading about. Not that you could call our life normal—not in the least, but we definitely didn't have any cool supernatural powers or anything like that. Still, fantasizing about it helped pass the endless miles down highways that look the same no matter where you are at. If I were a paranormal character, I would be an illusionist. I had made it an art form to never let anyone know how I was really feeling. We never knew what kind of mood my mom would be in from one day to the next, so most days I was the emotional catalyst of the family, always trying to appear happy and cheerful, when inside I was screaming. My brother, on the other hand, would be a special character. Kevin is a unique soul, caring and selfless. He definitely doesn't deserve this life—neither of us do, but at least we have each other, and I would die to protect him.

We arrived in Four Corners, Montana, in late September, over a full month after the school year had already started, but my little brother and I were used to that by now. The town definitely lived up to its name. Four adjacent corners with lonely looking establishments perched on each one. We observed the Higgins Grocers, which sounded vaguely familiar on the south corner and a small mom and pop restaurant called Sunny-Side Up on the corner directly across from it. Withers, a gas station that had seen better days, sat on the third corner opposite from the restaurant, which left the last corner to the run-down trailer park called Shady Lane that would be our new home.

As Jim, my "step-dork" as we liked to call him, pulled our beat-up car into the dirt-packed path, my brother Kevin and me exchanged horrified looks. We weren't freaked out we would be living in a trailer, since it was a humongo step-up from some of the dumps we had lived in over the years. Just the idea of having a roof over our heads was an absolute godsend. It was more the size of the town that made Kevin and I exchange uneasy glances. Even at nine, Kevin understood how our mom thought, and we both knew there was absolutely no way Lucinda would make it in a town this size.

Like always though, I kept my face impassive, not letting my disappointment show. It had taken most of the morning for Lucinda to sign all the housing papers the woman at the welfare office in Bozeman handed over. During that time, I'd allowed myself to daydream about the stability our lives would have, for at least a few months anyway, and after two weeks in a shelter, I was ready for a little space.

Living in a shelter was always tough on Kevin and me. The accommodations were always tight with no privacy to speak of with food that you ate just for the sake of eating. If I never drank another glass of powdered milk again, I would die a happy person.

This last shelter had been more bearable than most of the others we had lived in over the years. Instead of separating men and women into different spaces crammed with cots, they had family rooms that were roughly sixteen feet by sixteen feet where entire families could stay. The rooms had two double beds, which meant Kevin and I were forced to share. At seventeen, I should have bucked at the idea of sharing a room, let alone a bed with my brother, but

I wouldn't have had it any other way, he was all I had, and I've spent my entire life trying to protect him.

Already knowing that we would most likely only be living in our new home for a short while was always a hard pill to swallow, no matter how many times we'd been through this. It had taken us two weeks in the car to get to Montana from California since we had to make several pit stops to earn money for gas. Kevin and I were both equally sick of the car and didn't relish another move when Lucinda decided yet again that the grass was greener somewhere else.

Step-dork, Jim slowly drove past a string of mobile homes that varied in size and appearance. We'd stayed in our share of projects, dumpy motels and run-down apartments, but never a trailer park. I was surprised that some of them were actually relatively nice with extra built-on storm rooms and utility rooms. Small bushes and fake flowers bordered the majority of the homes, making it clear that the current owners took pride in the little plot of land they inhabited. I couldn't help but smile a little at the dozens of god-awful looking garden gnomes peeking out behind several of the bushes surrounding one of the trailers.

It all seemed so very normal, which only further proved our new home was doomed from the get-go. We definitely didn't exist in the realm of normal.

Jim pulled into a narrow drive and stopped in front of what was to be our new home. The overgrowth of weeds and unkempt bushes surrounding the trailer gave the indication that it had been sitting empty for quite a while. The exterior of the trailer was covered in faded metal paneling, but looked to be in decent enough shape. There were no broken windows as far as I could tell and as long as there were no holes in the floor or roof, it might actually be tolerable. Lucinda and Jim piled out of the vehicle, leaving Kevin and me behind in their typical parental-lacking fashion.

Kevin used his insignificant body weight to try to push the heavy car door open. The door cracked open slowly, sticking at half-mast on its rusty hinges. I twisted around on my seat and used my feet to push it open the rest of the way before sliding out after him. It would have made more sense for me to sit by the only door that opened in the back seat, but the rusted-out hole that took up the majority of the floorboard on my side of the car freaked Kevin out. He was scared he was going to fall through the floor, so I had taken the less desirable position for the remainder of the trip. Being older, I didn't want to admit to him that the hole sort of freaked me out too, especially at night when we were sleeping in the car. My mind would run wild, conjuring up images of every insect imaginable creeping up through the hole in the pitch-black night and crawling all over us. During the day, I would drape my bare feet out the open window, daydreaming about being somewhere else, anywhere else. This method worked through California and most of Nevada, but once we got into the mountain ranges, the temperature dropped drastically, making it impossible to keep the window open. Kevin and I stayed huddled together under the thin blanket we shared at night, shivering in our thin California apparel that didn't serve us well in the chillier temperatures we were driving through. Where the hole in the floor really sucked though was when the sleet and snow on the road splashed up from underneath the car. Kevin had a meltdown watching the snow spewing up through the hole, scared it wouldn't stop and would bury us alive in the backseat. My hands froze as I scooped it back up and made a game of throwing it back down in the hole. Kevin perked up at the makeshift game and admitted he even kind of missed it once we made our way down the mountain.

"So, should we go check out our new home?" I asked, using all my weight to close the stubborn car door behind me.

"I guess," he said grumpily.

"Hey, what's wrong?" I asked, using my hip to nudge him teasingly.

"Come on, look at this place, Katelyn. You know there's no way she's going to make it here," he muttered, kicking at a small pebble on the ground, making the dust swirl up and cover the toes of his worn-out sneakers.

"Hey, you never know. What do we always say?"

"That we're glass-half-full kind of people. It's not like I really know what that means," he said, still sulking.

"Yes you do. It means we believe in someday soon, right? Someday soon this crazy life will be behind us and we will hardly even remember any of this bad-crazy-messed-up stuff, okay?" I asked, pulling him in for a one-armed hug.

"Okay," he agreed, sliding one of his narrow arms around my waist as we headed up the metal stairs to our new home.

I pulled the door open and gasped when it opened easily making me take a steadying step backwards. I barely kept my balance, but poor Kevin who was standing directly behind me and weighs forty-five pounds soaking wet was knocked backwards, landing on his butt at the bottom of the stairs.

I couldn't stop the giggle that bubbled up my throat at his shocked expression. It had happened so fast, one minute he was standing behind me, and the next he was on his backside.

"Are you okay?" I asked, trying to control my giggles as he dusted off his backside.

"Yeah, but sheesh, keep your butt to yourself next time!" He said, racing up the three steps in front of me.

I followed behind him and together we stopped in the small living room, taking in our surroundings. I was pleasantly surprised that for something so small on the outside, it was somewhat spacious inside, but I guess anything would seem spacious after two weeks in a cramped shelter and another two camping out in a car.

The kitchen was at one end of the trailer and looked clean enough upon my inspection. The windows that lined the small kitchen space were covered with faded yellow curtains that could be closed at night for privacy. Underneath them stood a small oak table with two chairs which suited Kevin and my needs fine since Lucinda and Jim rarely ate with us.

The living room held a surprise that made Kevin squeal when he saw it. The television sitting on the rickety old stand was small in size and nothing like the HD TVs everyone had now, but going without television for months made us both appreciate having one, despite its lackluster appearance. The shelter we vacated that morning had a large flat screen in the common room that someone had donated, but since most of the other residents were women, talk shows and soap operas were pretty much on 24/7. Kevin had been missing his favorite cartoons for a while, but was careful not to mention it around Lucinda or Jim since they adamantly felt only babies watched cartoons.

Kevin flipped on the television quietly and settled down on the worn carpet in front of it. I smiled at him and continued to peruse the rest of the trailer. A small narrow hallway led out of the living room on the opposite side of the kitchen. Three doorways lined the hall and a fourth one stood at the end. Opening up the first door and glancing inside, I was pleased to see a small bedroom complete with a twin bed and a tall narrow dresser. Moving on to the next doorway, I discovered another small bedroom that mirrored the first one. Temporary or not, I couldn't help but feel giddy about having my own space in I don't know how long.

I continued my exploration through the rest of the trailer, finding a microscopic bathroom that at least had all the necessities, including a bathtub. I sighed with pleasure at the sudden luxuries we had.

Turning back around, I headed down the hallway, avoiding the room at the far end where Lucinda and Jim had disappeared to. By the grunting and moaning I had heard while I was inspecting the bathroom, I knew Mom and Jim would be busy for a while. Walking back into the first room I'd inspected, I decided to claim it as my own to further distance myself from the room on the end. I took time to inspect the dresser, opening each drawer in hopes that the last occupants had left something behind. I was mildly disappointed when I found them all empty with no hidden treasures. Still, I couldn't help but feel a little pleased as I sank onto the narrow bed, taking in my surroundings.

"All of this space is mine," I said quietly to myself. "I can close the door...." My private party was interrupted when I saw that my room had no door. Dismayed, I stood up to inspect it and grinned in delight when I discovered it was a pocket door. I pulled the small brass tab with my fingers and watched as the door slid out of the panel in the wall. "Sweet," I mumbled to myself, heading back toward the living room.

"Kevin, I'm going to go unload the car. Do you wanna help?" I asked my brother who was now lying across the sofa.

"Not really," he said meekly.

"You okay?" I asked, reaching up to brush my hand across his forehead.

"Yeah, just a little dizzy."

"It's probably because you're hungry. It's been hours since we ate breakfast at the shelter. Maybe if Mom comes out soon she'll give me the food stamp card she got this morning from that welfare lady. I'll go get some sandwich stuff at the grocery store," I said to him before I headed out to the car.

I opened up the trunk of the car with the keys, swearing under my breath at Lucinda. Skipping meals was a normal part of our life, but she swore she would try harder once the doctor at the clinic told her Kevin was failing to thrive. In layman's terms, it meant he wasn't gaining weight. The doctor had given her guidelines on the foods Kevin should be eating to help alleviate the problem, and Mom sat there, nodding her head in agreement, putting up a good front for the doctor, but as usual, her promises meant nothing. *Why can't she just try to make a freak'n effort for once*, I thought bitterly as I reached into the trunk and grabbed the duffle bag stacked on top. I grunted from its weight as I adjusted the strap around my narrow shoulder. Gripping the two handles together with my left hand, I tried to take some of the strain off my shoulder as I staggered toward the trailer. The bag was Lucinda's and was twice the size of all the other bags, making it a brute to carry.

"Hey, that looks heavy," a snarky voice said behind me.

Turning around, I saw that I was being studied intently by a girl that looked roughly to be around my age, but taller with flat brown hair that looked like it hadn't seen shampoo in days. She had high cheek bones that I would kill for, but her complexion was splotchy and greasy. Her dingy, baggy overalls, which I hadn't seen anyone wear in years, made her legs appear endless all the way down to her old dirty cowboy boots. I swept my eyes over her, seeing myself reflected back if not for the illusion I cloaked myself in.

She was poor like us and didn't care who knew it.

I was the exact opposite of her.

I had spent years perfecting the art of disguise. No one in the last ten or so schools I had attended over the past couple of years ever suspected by my appearance that most nights I slept in the car with my family, and that the majority of those nights we went to bed without dinner. I always washed carefully in the gas station restrooms each morning, taking care to make sure my hair was combed nicely and pulled back in a neat ponytail. I would tell myself that how we lived was no one's business and didn't matter, but I still kept my secret.

"Nah, it's not too bad," I said, adjusting the strap again, hoping she wouldn't volunteer to help.

"So, what grade are you in?" She asked in the same snotty tone as before.

"Um, I'm a senior. How about you?"

"Me too. I was supposed to graduate, but they held me back last year. Said they didn't think I was ready for that yet. I don't care much though, I wasn't looking forward to graduating yet anyways. My brother's been held back two years, so he'll be in our class too."

I cringed at the thought. *He'd been held back two years?* Each year it was a struggle for me to start midyear at a new school and try to keep up, but I somehow always managed to squeak by with passing grades by the end.

"Well, that's if we all get in the same class," I said, silently praying against the idea.

"Sure we will. There's only sixteen seniors in the whole school. Well, seventeen now with you."

"SEVENTEEN?" I asked shocked.

She laughed mockingly at my surprise. "Well, there's only fifteen ninth graders, so we got them beat. The second-grade class is the most this year though, they got nineteen."

"You mean the high school isn't separate?" I asked, feeling a little nauseous. The woman at the welfare office did mention that I would be going to a small school, but I hadn't given her words much thought, assuming that it would just be a smaller high school than I was used to. I never once considered this.

"Heck no, they group us all together like a herd of cattle. I've been going to Munford with the same group of people my whole life," she said with an edge in her voice that made it clear she held animosity against someone.

"Ugh, so it goes all the way down to kindergarten?" I asked, shuddering at the idea. The last school I attended in California was a regular high school, so being juniors, we had been part of the bigger fish group in the pond with the guppy freshmen and sophomores beneath us. I had secretly been looking forward to being at the top of the food chain this year, but it was a little much to think there would be tiny baby guppies swimming amongst us.

"Yep, and we ain't had a new student start since Shirley McJones moved here with her family six years ago.

13

Course, she had no problem fitting in since her father made millions in oil," she said with the same bite in her voice.

"There's no other school in this area?" I asked, searching for a lifeline.

"Nope, the closest schools are forty-five minutes away in Bozeman. With all the money some of the folks around here have, they could have bused us there, but noooo, they like the small feel of Munford and treat it more like a private school than a regular school. Of course, they still allow us peasants to attend," she said snidely.

"Well, I guess I better get this stuff inside," I said, edging toward the door, suddenly sick of all the new information I had just gained.

"Okay, well I'll see you at school," she said, turning on heel and shuffling away. I watched her kick at the dirt with the toe of her boot as she walked, making the loose dirt fly up and then fall back down covering her boots with a light dusting. Her shoulders seemed to slump from the weight of the large chip she obviously carried.

I gripped the handles of the duffle bag with one hand and pulled the door open with my free hand.

"What took so long?" Kevin asked as I dumped the oversized bag on the floor and sat next to him, gasping from the exertion I had used to haul everything inside.

"I met some girl that will be in my class at school," I muttered.

"How do you know she'll be in your class?" he asked puzzled.

"Because there's only like sixteen seniors in this whole school."

"Sixteen?"

"Yes," I said miserably as he started laughing.

"What are you laughing at, dweeb?" I said, a little annoyed that he found the situation funny.

"It's-s-s ju-just f-funny. I had more kids in my class last year," he said between his belly giggles.

"Ha-ha, keep laughing it up, punk," I said, affectionately ruffling his hair. It was nice to see him happy again. The last month of close quarters had been intense, and the strain had definitely worn on both of us.

"KATELYN," Lucinda yelled down the hall, making me cringe.

"Do you want me to go?" Kevin asked as I reluctantly got to my feet, looking down the hallway with trepidation.

"Nah, I got it. You watch your shows while you still have a chance."

I slowly made my way down the hall, dreading the idea of entering "their" new space.

"Yeah?" I asked through the thin door, hoping to delay entry into the room.

"We need our cigarettes," she said through the door with enough aggravation in her voice that it was clear I had taken too long to respond.

"Okay," I said, relieved it was an easy fix.

I quickly made my way down the hallway and down the steps to the car. I knew from past experience that not being prompt would only make matters worse for me in the long run. I had spent my entire life catering to my mother's whims and knew what was expected of me.

I grabbed both packs of cigarettes from the dashboard and the small empty tuna can they were using as an ashtray. I carried the cigarettes in one hand and the overflowing makeshift ashtray in the other up the three metal steps taking care not to let the used butts fall out of the can.

"Crap, I forgot their lighters," I mumbled, annoyed at myself as I pulled the door open.

"Kevin can you dump this in the trash while I grab the lighter out of the car," I asked, handing him the smelly ashtray.

"Sure," he said, cupping it in his small hand as I headed back down the stairs.

Within seconds, I headed back up the stairs and on my way down to their room. I knocked on the door lightly and held my breath as I slowly opened it. I was relieved to see that they were at least decent as they waited impatiently for their drug of choice.

"What took so long?" Lucinda demanded as I reached over to hand them their two different kinds of cigarettes.

"I forgot the lighter in the car and needed to dump the ashtray," I said passively, trying to get a gauge of her mood.

She shook her head. "Blondes. Always forgetful," she joked with Jim.

"Yep, I'm surprised she remembered which trailer we're in," he said, choking on his own laughter at his stupid joke.

I ignored both of their jokes, knowing the best move was to let their comments roll off my back. There was a time when I would have killed myself trying to win Lucinda's approval, but years of physical and verbal abuse had hardened me and my only goal now was to protect Kevin from the same abuses I endured.

"I brought your bag in from the car. Do you want me to go over to the store after I finish unloading the rest of the stuff?" I asked, addressing Lucinda since most time Jim was incapable of making trivial decisions.

"Sure, that sounds good. Rosa, our welfare rep, said the trailer was stocked with basic stuff, so I'm sure we have pots and pans. Buy the stuff for sloppy burritos, and I'll make dinner tonight," she said, proud of the commitment she had made.

"Sure Mom, that sounds good," I said, my mouth already watering at the thought. For all her faults, she was definitely a great cook and when she got the inclination to make something homemade, it was always guaranteed to be tasty. "Is it okay if I get lunch stuff for school tomorrow, too?"

She grimaced at my words. "I guess, but you better get the forms you need for free lunches. I don't want to be wasting our money when the state owes us."

"Okay Mom," I said, backing up out of the room before she changed her mind. I hated asking for the forms at school and going to a small school would make it even worse.

I had just barely closed their door behind me when I heard Lucinda's voice calling me back through the thin wall. Sighing, I turned back around.

"Yeah?" I asked, opening the door a crack.

"Bring me my makeup bag and clothes before you go off gallivanting around."

"And I want a big glass of ice water," Jim piped in, not wanting to miss out on handing out a task.

I looked at Lucinda inquiringly, but she let it slide. She was usually picky when Jim or any of the other step-whatevers tried to boss me around. She felt her demands were justified since she was my actual flesh and blood, but Jim was just a step-dad in a long string of losers Kevin and I had to endure over the last ten years. Lucinda liked to switch husbands like most women switched handbags or shoes. The cycle was always the same. They would meet, fall in love promptly, realize they knew nothing about each other, and fight until Lucinda gave them the boot. The fighting I could endure, but the love part was always nauseating since most of the time she didn't care who was around when they groped each other. I was six when I learned what the "birds and the bees" were and decided at that moment I wanted no part of that if it made you act so crazy. It was several years later that I realized that not all adults flaunted their sex life so openly and the majority of them didn't act like loons over it.

"Sure," I said to Jim, not wanting to rock the boat.

I unloaded the rest of the car in my usual methodical way, placing our meager belongings in their appropriate places.

I delivered Lucinda's makeup bag to her just as she requested. Her makeup bag was a long standing joke with Kevin and me, since she treated it like it was the Holy Grail. She once left one of my step-dweebs on the side of the road when he threw it out the window during an argument. It took Kevin and me almost an hour to pick up the makeup that had scattered across the landscape. Lucinda cursed out the dope the entire time as Kevin and I tried to salvage as much of the busted up cosmetics as we could. Once we had it all cleaned up, we pulled away, leaving step-dad number four looking forlorn on the side of the road. Looking out the back window, I had almost felt sorry for the poor guy. Lucinda suffered the seven stages of grief over the next three hundred miles we traveled and contemplated turning around multiple times, but by the time we reached the next big city and started to settle in, he was soon forgotten as Lucinda searched for her next Prince Charming. I often yearned for those brief three months when it had just been the three of us. Lucinda was a much better parental figure when she wasn't fawning over her newest obsession.

Chapter 2

I headed over to Higgins Grocers once everything was unpacked from the car. Relishing the rare treat of being completely by myself, I kept my pace slow as I made my through the trailer park. We had never lived in a community like this and I was amazed at the amount of work each owner put into their makeshift homes. My favorite was the yard that held the multiple garden gnomes. Most of them were cheesy and quite ugly, but I liked the idea that they took the time to collect things they enjoyed. I've never had a collection of anything. I tried with books, many times over, but each time we moved, everything that wouldn't fit in a duffle bag was left behind. I did manage to hold onto three of my favorite books over the years. They were all falling apart from being read over and over again, but they were by far my most treasured items. I always hid them in the bottom of my bag so Lucinda wouldn't make me dump them. The only thing she and I had in common, except for the obvious mother-daughter thing, was a deep love of reading, but she felt books were disposable and easily replaced. I felt the exact opposite. Each book I read opened up a whole new world for me. It didn't matter that we were poor, had no food or no place to sleep. If the story was good enough, I could completely submerge myself into the pages, letting the outside world fade away.

I was pleased to find the grocery store clean and well lit inside. It was a little smaller than I expected, but seemed to be fully stocked. Grabbing a buggy from the front of the store, I slowly made my way up and down the aisles, grabbing the ingredients for lunches and dinners that were cheap enough to keep Lucinda pacified.

I made sure to scoop up a dozen packages of Top O' Ramen soup for Kevin and me. At twenty cents a package, it was a cheap staple item for us. We didn't always have a means to cook them, so we would crunch the package up, pour the seasoning mix into the bag of broken pieces and shake it up. That was Kevin's favorite part. We would munch on it with a peanut butter and jelly sandwich and it would fill our bellies for hours afterwards.

As I pushed the cart down the cereal aisle, I passed all the name brands that Kevin and I preferred, choosing the generic economy-sized bags instead. Some of them didn't hold a candle to the name brands, but we had learned through trial and error that the generic chocolate puffs were the closest in taste to Cocoa Puffs. I grabbed one of the bags from the back knowing they usually moved the older stock to the front. We could tolerate the generic brand, but once it went stale, it really sucked.

Milk and orange juice were the next items to make it into my cart. I dreaded the weight they would add to the bags on the walk home, but knew both were necessities to Kevin's diet. Once I had all my items, I pulled my buggy off to the side to total up my cart and cringed at the amount. I surveyed the cart critically, trying to decide what I could put back to shave seven dollars off my total. I remember Rosa telling Lucinda there was three hundred-seventy-five dollars on the card, but I also knew from past experience that overspending would not go over well. I put back Kevin's Cosmic Brownies along with the grapes and bananas I was hoping to sneak into his lunch. Kevin and I weren't huge fans of fruit since we really didn't have much opportunity to add them to our diet, but I had wanted to start encouraging him to eat healthier. I noticed most of the produce was unusually costly here, but figured it must be off-season or something.

By the time I made my way to the front of the store, the sun was starting to set outside, so I quickly unpacked my goods onto the conveyor belt. I was so intent on my task that I was startled when I realized the bag boy was talking to me.

"Huh?" I asked looking up. My face filled with color as I took in his boyishly handsome face. He had thick brown hair that threatened to fall in his eyes if not for the hand he used to push it back off his forehead. His eyes were the typical brown you would expect, but seemed to sparkle as he smiled at me. Within our endless travels over the years, I had run across my share of cute boys, and even went out with a few, but it was the dimples that sat in both corners of his mouth that instantly captivated me and set him apart from any other boy I had ever met. He was more than boyishly cute, the word *steamy* jumped to mind. I knew without a shadow of doubt he was trouble.

"I said you must be new," he said, smiling broadly at me.

"Yeah, we just moved in across the way," I said, indicating the trailer park across the street.

"That's great. We never get new people around here. The last people to move here was Shirley Mc..."

"Jones," I finished for him.

"Exactly. How did you know that?"

"I met some girl earlier and she filled me in."

"Brown hair, crazy tall, has a brother?" he asked.

"Yep, that would be her, except I didn't meet the brother."

"That would be Bethany and her brother Matt," he said in a tone that was hard to place.

I looked at him wondering what the issue was, instantly suspecting it had something to do with her attire.

I turned my attention back to the less-than-friendly cashier as she scanned my items, deciding right then and there he was way out of my league.

"We're all in the same class," he continued. "Though they don't like the rest of us all that much," he added.

"Why not?" I asked, trying to sound disinterested.

"Not sure," he replied, shrugging slightly. "Are you a junior or a senior?" He asked, changing the subject.

"Senior, and I have to admit, it's wigging me out a little that we will be in the same school with a bunch of munchkins," I said, grimacing.

He threw back his head and laughed.

"It's not as bad as it sounds, they keep us pretty separated."

"So, is this the only job around here?" I asked, hoping for the opportunity to finally get a job.

"Pretty much. My dad owns the store, so I was a shoo-in," he said, looking slightly embarrassed. "I could put a word in for you if you would like?" he said, shooting me one of his knee-melting-palm-sweating-dimpled smiles.

"Um, that's okay." I replied, not entirely crazy about being indebted to him.

"You sure? It's no prob, my dad's a fair boss and such."

"That's okay, but it's cool you have a built-in job."

"Yeah, well, he kind of owns a bunch of stores, but we live close to this one so I'm pretty much slave labor since he's actually just grooming me for the fu-"

"How did you want to pay?" An impatient voice asked, interrupting him.

"Oops, sorry," I said, turning back to the slightly aggravated sales clerk. "Um, with this," I said, trying not to let it show that I was bothered about paying with my mom's food stamp card. I shifted my body to the side so I wasn't facing the cute bag boy that was making my pulse act erratically.

"Are you Lucinda Richards?" she asked, reading my mom's name off the card.

"No, that's my mom," I said, wishing that the floor would open up and swallow me whole so I could escape. Even a meteor crashing through the roof would have been preferred.

"Then your mom will have to come in and sign for it," she said almost gleefully, enjoying the fact that she was putting me on the spot.

"I never had a problem before," I said coolly in an effort to cover my embarrassment. Being poor was definitely not fun at times.

"Marge, I'm sure it's okay," the bag boy said, coming to my rescue.

"Maybe I should call the manager to check," she said in a defiant voice.

"Marge, my dad owns the store and I said it's okay," he said in a voice that left no argument.

"Fine, but if I get in any trouble, I'm telling your father you approved it," she said, clearly aggravated at being trumped by a seventeen-year-old.

I kept my head held high, trying to act like the entire confrontation hadn't mortified me. Paying with the food stamp card was always embarrassing, but the majority of the time the stores were so busy no one paid much attention to you.

I met my rescuer's eyes dead-on, feeling completely vulnerable as he seemed to peer through my defenses.

"These bags seem pretty heavy. Do you want me to carry them for you?" he asked, not quite releasing them completely to me as our hands touched.

"No, I got 'em," I said. "I'm tougher than I look," I added, making it clear I didn't need his help. I pulled on the handles until he reluctantly released them.

"Are you sure?" he asked one last time.

I nodded. "I'm used to it," I said, feeling the mask that was hiding my embarrassment begin to slip as he studied me intently.

"Okay," he surrendered, sounding a little disappointed.

I gripped the handles tightly making my knuckles turn white. His now sympathetic gaze was enough to wither the tough-girl front I was trying to portray, so I turned quickly, fleeing from the store before I completely crumbled.

I didn't slow my pace as I continued to berate myself all the way back to the entrance of the trailer park. Some master of illusion I was. We're not even here one day and in one fell swoop I'd allowed a swoon-worthy hunk a glimpse into my reality. The thought of facing him again the next day made my stomach flip. For a moment I wanted to be selfish as I contemplated using Lucinda's spontaneity in my favor by harping on the smallness of the town. I knew if I worded it right I could convince her we should move on and leave the small town behind. Kevin's face floated through my head and I imagined his disappointment if we packed it in and hit the road again. I had promised him I would try to keep us in this place as long as I could. Could I betray him by breaking my promise just because I was afraid that some cute guy had caught a small glimpse of the real me?

I knew I couldn't do that to him. After our last bout of homelessness, Kevin needed some semblance of stability, for as long as it would last anyway.

By tomorrow I would have my mask firmly back in place. Avoiding grocery boy would be tough in a small school, but hopefully he would turn out to be a halfway decent guy and not make me the front page news. Satisfied with my plan of action, I tried to make my mind forget about him and not think about his yummy eyes or dimples that made my palms sweat. In a different life I could see myself with someone like him, but here and now, we're just from different worlds and had no place together. It was for the best anyway. I had no desire to start up a relationship with some guy when my days here were numbered. I just wanted to make a few friends and enjoy our temporary home while it lasted. Making friends was never hard for me even though I was always shy initially. Lucinda, during one of her kinder moments, had once told me that I had the gift for putting people at ease and that they automatically gravitated to me because of it.

Tomorrow we would see if she was right.

***

Kevin was waiting for me on the top step when I finally staggered to the trailer.

"What are you doing out here?" I asked.

"They're fighting," he said, not needing to elaborate.

"Ugh, are you sure?" I asked, seeing our chance of a decent dinner slowly slipping away.

"Yeah, they were quiet at first, but they've gotten louder."

"Well, crap," I muttered, trying to come up with a game plan. "Why don't you go sit in the car since it's chilly out here? I'll go see how bad it is."

He nodded, heading to the car. We both hated when Lucinda fought with whomever she was hooked up with because the fights always seemed to turn volatile. Kevin

29

hated the fights because the yelling hurt his ears. I hated them because most times they turned physical, and I hated having to step in. Getting hit was not my idea of a fun time, but more often than not I always got caught in the crossfire. It was one thing to suffer Lucinda's wrath if I pissed her off, but it really sucked to get caught in a fight that had nothing to do with me.

I could hear the yelling before I even opened the door. They were still in their room which was a good sign for me. Rushing to the kitchen, I threw the groceries in the cupboards and fridge as the yelling escalated. I hastily pulled out the peanut butter and jelly and hurriedly assembled a couple sandwiches each for Kevin and me. Once they were made, I snatched up sandwich bags and two of the packages of Top Ramen soup. Stowing it all in one of the now-empty grocery bags, I linked my wrist through the handle of the bag leaving my hands free to pour a tall glass of milk for us to share. With dinner in hand, I quietly made my way to my room to grab the blanket off my bed and the book I had laid out earlier. My plans for lying in my own bed reading would have to wait.

I scurried back down the hall with my arms full, almost home free when their fight spilled out of their room. Jim knocked into me as he rushed toward the front door, making me spill milk everywhere. "Your mother's a fuck'n psycho," he yelled on his way out the door. I groaned silently. He would pay for that comment.

Sure enough, not a moment after he slammed the door, Lucinda flew out of her room like a bat out of hell. "PSYCHO?" she screamed at the closed door as she rushed to get by me. I knew I was in for it the moment she saw the spilt milk on the floor. "And what the hell are you doing?" She screeched, swinging out at me. The blow landed before I could think of something that would pacify her. My head jerked back from the impact across my left cheek.

"It was an accident," I said, keeping my voice even as I cupped my stinging cheek with my now free hand.

"Well, clean it up and stop standing there like a moron!" she screamed, turning her rage toward me.

"Okay, Lucin...uh, Mom," I said correcting myself, hoping she wouldn't notice my slip.

I mopped up the milk with toilet paper I had grabbed from the bathroom since we didn't have any paper towels. In my haste to clean up the mess quickly, the toilet paper became a soggy mess. I knew logically I should have grabbed an empty grocery bag, but my head was still fuzzy from the hit. I didn't realize my mistake until I was carrying the soggy toilet paper to the kitchen trash, leaving little droplets of milk that slipped between my cupped hands splattering onto the linoleum floor.

"KATELYN, you stupid ass, you're dripping milk all over the damn place!" Lucinda screamed at me as I dropped to my knees to clean up the drops of milk. Lucinda's rage hit the optimal level as she pelted me over and over again with her closed fist. The blows fell heavy on my back and head. I curled up in a ball, waiting for the storm to pass. I knew it would be over soon and that when it passed her rage would be gone. That was the way it always played out, Lucinda hit until she was done being mad.

After a few moments, she finally left me on the floor as she stormed out of the trailer. I waited several moments to make sure she wasn't coming back before uncurling my aching body. My head pounded in agony and my back tried to boycott my movements, but after a moment, I was finally able to rise.

I looked up and saw Kevin standing in the hallway with tears streaming down his cheeks.

"It's okay, champ," I said, grimacing in pain as I tried to smile to reassure him it was okay.

"I could've stopped her," he said, looking at me defiantly.

"No, you couldn't, and you know that," I told him sternly. I had drilled it into his head repeatedly, never to interfere. As a rule, Lucinda never really hit him and I didn't want her to get any ideas. I could take the punishment, but there was no way Kevin was going to.

"Are you okay?" Kevin asked, accepting my rules once again.

"Sure, it barely hurts at all. She could hardly get a good angle with me hunched on the floor like that," I lied easily.

32

Kevin wiped the tears off his cheeks and looked relieved at my words.

"I made us sandwiches," I said, picking up the now crushed bag on the floor. "Why don't you get us more milk while I use the bathroom, and then we'll eat in my room like a slumber party, okay?"

Kevin smiled at my words, "Okay," he said, scurrying off to the kitchen to get our milk.

I gingerly picked up the rest of the stuff off the floor and lugged it back to my room before heading to the bathroom. I closed the bathroom door firmly behind me and turned the water on full blast as the shakes completely consumed me. I did not cry since I had a strict rule to never let Kevin see me cry. I'd learned to shut most of my emotions away, but at times like this, my emotional wall would crumble slightly. I wrapped my arms around my midsection as I sank down on the closed toilet seat. Getting the shakes after one of Lucinda's meltdowns was the only reaction I couldn't seem to control. Once they took hold, it was all I could do to remain upright. The pain from the multiple blows was insignificant versus the fear that always raced through me during one of her rages. I loathed admitting that Lucinda scared me. I was terrified that one day her rage would not be pacified and she would hit until there was nothing left, leaving Kevin behind, alone.

After a few moments, I finally pulled myself together, knowing that Kevin would start to worry. I stood on shaky legs in front of the sink and studied my reflection in the mirror. My left cheek looked like I had gone way overboard with the blush, making it resemble half of a clown's face. I touched it gingerly and grimaced in pain. It was tender, but looked like it wouldn't bruise, which was a relief. I turned and lifted my shirt to see if I could get a glimpse of the damage to my back. I could only see a small section, but saw several bruises were already starting to form. Ugh, it would be painful to sit in a desk chair all day tomorrow. I would have to make sure I was careful not to lean back, or it would only make the bruises worse.

Turning back around, I cupped cool water in my hands and splashed it on my face. The temperature stung my sensitive skin, but I knew that the coldness would help the mark on my cheek that would only upset Kevin further. After several more soakings, the puffiness around my cheek seemed to dissipate somewhat, and I didn't look quite as scary. Using the towel off the rack, I dried up all the water off the laminate counter and straightened up the bathroom before I headed back to my room.

"What took so long?" Kevin asked worriedly as I closed the pocket door behind me.

"Hey, just girl stuff," I said, trying to ease his mind.

Wise beyond his years, he studied me critically before answering. "You sure?" he finally asked.

"I'm sure, punk," I said affectionately, sliding back on my bed so I could prop myself up gingerly against the headboard. "Let's eat. I'm famished," I said once I was as comfortable as I was going to get.

Kevin smiled, crawling up next to me. He opened the bag and distributed the now flattened sandwiches as I crunched up our dry soup and poured it into clear sandwich bags. I tore the corner of the seasoning packet open with my mouth and dumped the contents in the bag. Sealing it up tightly, I handed it over to Kevin so he could shake it up. I made quick work out of the second soup package, and we were soon eating.

Glancing at my watch, I was dismayed to see that it was already past eight. *Nothing like waiting twelve hours to eat,* I thought wryly as Kevin wolfed his meal down with gusto. We polished off the milk and threw all our trash in the empty grocery bag and settled back on my bed. Within seconds, Kevin's eyes became heavy and he drifted off to sleep. I fought to keep mine open, but the turmoil of the evening had taken its toll on me and they slowly started to drift closed.

My eyes jerked open several hours later when I heard my bedroom door being slid open. I watched as Lucinda tiptoed in quietly. The storm had passed and I could see the remorse on her face.

"I'm really sorry I hit you, Katelyn," she said quietly, being careful not to wake Kevin.

"I know, Mom," I whispered back.

"I just got so angry when I saw you had dumped milk all over the floor when we just barely got here."

"I know, Mom," I repeated, not bothering to tell her that Jim had bumped into me during their fight. By her passive behavior, I could tell they had made up, and it would do me no good to point a finger.

"You just have to be careful. We don't know if the state will come check up on this place since they're letting us stay here. Remember what happened in Texas."

"I know, I'm sorry. I'll be more careful," I said, not daring to point out that we had gotten kicked out of the housing in Texas when she designated herself the neighborhood animal rescuer, letting the entire house be overrun with strays she kept taking in.

"And I'll try not to let myself get so angry at your mistakes," she said. "Do you want me to take him to his bed?" she asked as an afterthought, indicating Kevin.

"Nah, he's okay. He can try his new room out tomorrow."

"Okay, I'll see you in the morning."

"Night," I said, reaching over to switch on my travel alarm as she turned off the bedroom light on her way out.

"It wasn't your fault the milk spilled," Kevin whispered quietly in the dark.

"I know, but at least she's happy again. She just feels bad that she hit me and needs it to be for a reason," I said, trying to justify her actions.

"I hate her when she hits you."

"No, you don't. You just don't like it," I said, scolding him softly.

"Why do you defend her?"

"Because she's our mom, if we don't defend her, who will?"

"Well, I still don't like her to hit you," he added stubbornly.

"I know, but better me than you with your chicken arms," I joked, reaching over to pinch his arm softly.

"Very funny, sis. One of these days I'm going to grow up, and then we'll see," he mumbled, drifting back off to sleep.

"I hope so," I said softly to his sleeping form, pulling the blanket up over us before I drifted off to sleep.

Chapter 3

My alarm startled me awake the next morning as I lay shivering under the thin blanket Kevin and I were sharing; *I love the little guy, but man is he a bed hog*, I thought, watching him curled up in a tight ball. Taking care not to wake him yet, I painfully climbed out of bed with my sore back protesting my every move.

Having no carpet and no heat made the cold linoleum floor feel like ice against my bare feet. With a clean shirt and my zip-up hoodie in hand, I headed to the bathroom for a shower. I cranked the knob to the hottest setting to let water heat up a bit before stepping inside. Every new bump and bruise throbbed as I slipped out of the t-shirt and jeans I wore to bed last night. After several moments under the soothing water, the chills I had been fighting began to subside. I allowed myself the luxury of a longer shower knowing the hot water would go a long way in easing the pain in my back.

I reluctantly shut off the water when the temperature began to cool and stepped out into the steamy bathroom. Wrapping the only towel I could find in the trailer around my midsection, I swiped my hand across the small medicine cabinet mirror and studied my reflection. The mark on my face had faded significantly, which was a relief. A little foundation would lighten it further.

The cooler air from the rest of the trailer began to seep into the bathroom, causing me to shiver slightly. I stepped back into my only pair of jeans and my clean shirt and hoodie. Finally somewhat warm, I was able to finish getting ready.

By the time I left the bathroom, Kevin and Mom were up, and I could hear them chatting in the kitchen.

"And a new backpack?" I heard Kevin ask.

"Yep, you would get a new backpack, too," Mom said, looking much more mellowed than she had the day before.

"What's going on?" I asked, pouring myself a glass of milk.

"Mom said we get to go to the thrift store to pick out school clothes, and she has a voucher so we can get school supplies from some bank."

I looked at her questioningly.

"I guess one of the banks in Bozeman did a school supply drive this year and they still have stuff left," she said, lighting up a cigarette. "They gave us a voucher for three hundred dollars for your school clothes and other stuff at some thrift store. If there's any left, maybe you can get some books, too," she said, offering an olive branch.

"That would be good," I said, munching on a piece of toast. As a rule, I always accepted the olive branch Lucinda would hold out. Holding a grudge wasn't in my nature, and each day brought its own set of challenges already, so holding onto past hurts would have only bogged me down.

"Okay, good. I'll pick you guys up after school, but starting tomorrow you'll be busing it," she said.

"Yay, I get to ride the bus with Katelyn," Kevin said, bouncing up in his chair.

"Oh joy," I said, ruffling his hair on the way back to my room.

I made my bed, making a mental note to remember blankets when went to the thrift store later.

***

The drive to school was short and before I knew it, Lucinda was pulling our dumpy car in between two oversized SUVs that looked brand spanking new.

"Wow, this looks like something the president would ride in," Kevin said, gawking at the large black Ford Expedition off to his right. I smiled. Kevin was obsessed with the President of the United States and referred often to him.

Walking around to his side of the car, I had to agree with him. The vehicle was very imposing with its jet-black paint job, chrome trim and wheels, and tinted windows.

40

"Sheesh, I wonder who drives that," I said as we trailed behind Lucinda toward the front door of the school.

I sighed with pleasure when we stepped into the lobby where the heat enveloped us, warding off the chill from outside. Judging by our surroundings, I could tell right off the bat this was going to be unlike any school we'd ever attended. Gone were the industrial light blue walls, buzzing fluorescent lights and scarred laminate countertops I was used to. Soothing taupe-colored walls were broken up by rich maple chair rails that ran the perimeter of the oversized space. Granite countertops and hardwood floors completed the warm inviting look. Twelve large bulletin boards hung around the room and judging by the decorations on them, there was one for each grade level.

"May I help you?" A kind elderly woman asked Lucinda.

"Yeah, I need to sign my two kids up," Lucinda said, nodding her head in our direction.

"That's lovely, dear. I'm sure you two are going to love this school," she said, addressing us.

"I wouldn't be too sure of that," Lucinda said, voicing my thoughts in her usual abrasive way.

The woman looked a little surprised at Lucinda's tone, or maybe it was her comment.

"It's a little odd keeping all these kids together in one school, don't you think?" Lucinda asked, reaching in her bag for her pack of cigarettes.

I looked away embarrassed. Lucinda absolutely hated that people could tell her where she could and couldn't smoke. Being one to buck the system at every opportunity available, she always tried to light up anywhere and everywhere.

"Oh, there's no smoking in the building or on school property," the woman said, all kindness disappearing from her voice as she looked at Lucinda reproachfully.

"Right, of course not," Lucinda said sarcastically, dropping her cigarettes back into her bag.

I kept my eyes everywhere but on Lucinda and the woman who I knew was now probably judging us. This was nothing new to me.

The door behind us opened up letting in a gust of cold air. Relieved to finally have something to look at, I turned to see who had entered the room, and nearly groaned out loud when I saw it was the swoon-worthy-dimple boy, as I had come to think of him. *OMG, could this get any worse?* I couldn't help thinking to myself.

Oblivious to my discomfort, he shot me the same dimpled smile from the night before as he walked around the granite countertop. "Hi, Mrs. Johnson, how are you doing this morning?" he said, grabbing a stack of papers off the counter in front of her. He sorted through them for a moment before distributing them in the appropriate cubbies.

"Great, Max, how about you?" she asked in a lighter tone.

"The same. School, work, school, slave labor, you know how it is," he said, shooting her a smile.

"You tell your father to stop working you so hard, or I'll have to stage some kind of grocery store boycott," she said, trying to sound stern.

"You know it won't do any good, Mrs. Johnson. Anytime I even think about griping, I get to hear about how he had to walk through like ten feet of snow, ten miles each way to school every day," Max said, laughing easily with her.

I knew I should look away, but there was something captivating about the way he laughed with such abandon. His laughter was so warm and contagious. I could feel the corners of my own mouth pulling up to smile in response. I looked down hastily so he wouldn't get the wrong idea.

"Do you need me to do anything else before I head off for class?"

"Actually, would you mind walking these new students to their classes? Kevin here should be in Ms. Davis's class and let's see, oh, and Katelyn will be in Mr. Graves's class with you. Well, that makes it easy," she said, shooting a smile my way.

"Sure, no prob," he said, turning to Kevin and me. "Ready?"

"Yeah," Kevin said enthusiastically.

43

"Um, sure," I answered, looking back at Lucinda who was busy filling out our registration papers. Part of me was anxious to flee in case she did anything else embarrassing, while another part of me wanted to stay so I could try to keep her in line and out of trouble.

Kevin and Max made the decision for me by heading out into the hallway beyond the front office.

"This way is the elementary section," Max said, walking us down a wide hallway painted a warm sunshine yellow. Doorways lined the hall with floor to ceiling double glass walls that broke up the space in between the doorways, giving a bird's eye view of the landscape beyond the building.

"The building is simple enough," Max explained as we walked. The very last classroom down this hall is kindergarten and it opens up onto the playground. Next to that is the first grade class, then the second grade class, and so on. We get the other side of the building, and ours opens up to the basketball hoops and ski trails we use."

"Ski trails?" I asked puzzled.

"Yeah. During November, December, and January they take us out cross-country skiing all the time for P.E."

"Wow! Me too?" Kevin asked happily.

"Yep, you too, buddy. It's kind of a school rule. You have to have a really good doctor's note to get out of it.

"Why would you want to?" Kevin asked, clearly confused.

"Oh believe me, there's plenty of times you don't feel like going out and freezing you're a... butt," he said, quickly correcting himself.

"Oh you can say ass, I hear it all the time."

"Kevin!" I said, shooting him a warning look.

"Oops, sorry, Katelyn," he said, looking instantly remorseful. He knew speaking about our home life with others was taboo.

Max looked at us puzzled, but I ignored him.

"So, is this Kevin's class?" I asked, pointing to the door we had stopped in front of.

"Huh? Oh, right. Yeah, this is Ms. Davis's class," he answered, pulling the door open so we could enter.

Kevin's teacher, Ms. Davis, was busy writing on the dry erase board that lined the front of the classroom. She was barely five foot tall and I wouldn't say she was chunky, she just looked more round than if she would have been a foot taller. She did have cute, short blonde hair that was cut in a flattering style that framed and enhanced her face. Her most striking attribute was her blue eyes which seemed to sparkle like the ocean would if the sun was hitting it.

She looked over as the three of us entered the room.

"Ms. Davis, this is Kevin and his sister Katelyn," Max said, introducing us.

"It's a pleasure to have you Kevin," she said, bustling over to us as her hips knocked into the desks in the front

45

row. "We're going to have a fun and entertaining year together," she said in a warm bubbling voice that instantly put Kevin at ease.

I smiled in relief, feeling comfortable that Kevin would be in good hands. Glancing around his room, I was almost envious that I couldn't stay when I saw the inviting interactive centers that were spaced around the room, including a comfy book nook that sat in the far corner surrounded by books and comfortable throw pillows.

"Okay punk, I'll see you after school," I said affectionately, giving Kevin a light tap on the arm before Max and I left the room.

"This school's something else," I said to Max after a few awkward moments of silence.

"Yeah, I guess it's nice here, but aren't all schools pretty much like this?" Max asked.

"Really?" I asked sarcastically. "Try not at all. Do you ever watch TV?"

"Sure, but if I believed everything I saw on TV there'd be vampires and werewolves running around everywhere," he said, shooting me another one of his dimpled smiles.

"True," I said grinning, forgetting that I was supposed to be keeping my distance from him. "But at least they're not bad to look at," I teased.

He threw his head back and laughed. "You got me there," he said when he finally stopped laughing.

"So, how do you guys survive out here so far from any fast food places or movie theaters?"

"Well, there's a McDonald's about fifteen miles up the road, off the main highway. Movies, on the other hand, are another story. It has to be a real blockbuster for us to make the long drive to the city. Usually, we'll all hang out at my house or my buddy Clint's. We both have big TVs so it's all cool."

"Hmmm," I said a bit skeptically.

"Trust me, you can come hang with us sometime and see," he said as he stopped in front of a door at the opposite end of the long hallway. "Ta-da, this is us," he said, enthusiastically opening the door.

Max held the door wide open so I could step into the brightly, lit, room. All sound suddenly evaporated as every eye in the room pivoted toward us. I forced myself to keep from staring uncomfortably at the floor, trying not to look too embarrassingly flush as I felt everyone studying me like a lab rat. Being new was an old hat for me.

"Making your own hours, Maxwell?" the teacher asked good-naturedly, breaking the silence.

Max laughed, "Nah, not this time. Mrs. Johnson asked me if I would take Katelyn here and her brother to their classes," Max said coolly, obviously sharing a good rapport with the teacher.

"Katelyn is it? Well, it's a pleasure to meet you. Welcome to our crazy class," he said, spreading his hands out to indicate the students who were sitting behind their desks throughout the room.

"Um, thanks," I said, responding to his laid back demeanor. He reached out to shake my hand, and I couldn't help returning his welcoming smile. He instantly eased my tension, which was a rarity for me on the first day of school. Perhaps it was the kind laugh lines in the corners of his eyes or the plentiful amount of grey hairs lining his head, beard and mustache, but something about him instantly engaged me.

"How about you share a desk with—" he paused as he scanned the room. "Rebecca, just until we can get you one of your own from the storage room. Rebecca, raise your hand so Katelyn can join you," he said, pointing out a tall girl in the back of the room. "Clint, do me a favor and grab Katelyn my desk chair for now."

"Sure thing, Mr. Graves," a curly, blond haired kid answered, shooting a cocky grin my way as he passed.

None of this was new territory for me. The way we moved, Kevin and I usually attended at least three schools a year. I was used to being gawked at on my arrival, but I was beginning to realize this time would be way different since the school was so small.

"Here you go," he said, setting my chair down next to the pretty girl the teacher had indicated.

"Hi, I'm Rebecca," the girl next to me said, introducing herself.

"Katelyn," I said, shooting her a shy smile.

"That's Alicia and Shirley," she said, pointing to the two girls who were sitting at the desk on each side of us.

"Hi," I said, scoping them out. Their designer clothes and handbags clued me in that they obviously had money, and were probably part of the popular crowd here.

"Alright girls, introductions for the rest of the class will have to wait until later. We have a date with Ms. Higgins," Mr. Graves said, mysteriously holding up a book I had never seen before.

Confused, I looked around to see if the rest of the class had their own copies, assuming the book he held was part of our course reading.

"Katelyn, I just started this book earlier this week, but you should be able to catch up with the storyline easily enough," Mr. Graves said, sitting down on a tall stool at the front of the room.

Before I could begin to catalog my astonishment, he began to read from the book he held in his hand. Looking around, I saw all the students watching him with rapt attention. It had been years since I had seen a teacher read out loud to the class, and I was instantly captivated at the idea. Sitting back in my temporary seat, I let myself forget everything but the words that were being read aloud to us. His voice was rich and his pronunciation of the words made the pages come alive. I was soon wrapped up completely in the mystery of the story and silently encouraged him to read faster.

All too soon, he closed up the book and it was time for us to move on to our next subject. I was grossly disappointed to see him put the book aside, but as the day wore on, I realized that in every subject he taught, he exhibited the same engaging attitude that made you want to pay attention to everything he said.

The morning quickly passed as we moved through lessons in English and science. Thanks to the friendliness of Rebecca and her friends, I didn't feel nearly as lost as I normally did on a first day of class. Before I knew it, it was lunch time.

"Don't we go to the cafeteria?" I asked as Rebecca and her friends pushed their desks together.

"No, we don't have a cafeteria," Alicia, one of Rebecca's friends said wishfully. "I wish we did though, it seems like it would be kinda fun. We could have, like, a salad bar with everything on it," she bubbly continued.

"Trust me, you're not missing out," I said as they looked at me skeptically. "No seriously, they're always crazy loud, overly crowded and depending what the cook is making, the smells don't usually mix well with a bunch of kids all crammed into one space."

Everyone around me busted out laughing, making me flush at the sudden attention I was getting.

"Seems like you've had plenty of experience," Max said as he and the blond guy, Clint, and another tall guy, whose name I didn't know pushed their desks up against the backside of ours, creating a rectangular shaped table.

"Oh yeah, you could say that," I said lightly, not delving into just how much experience I did have with different cafeterias.

After that, the conversation around our makeshift table flowed light and easy as my new friends peppered me with questions about my last school. I kept my answers humor-filled and centered them on the last school I had attended in California. Once I mentioned it was in California, they were instantly star struck. I didn't bother to point out that the state was huge and the section we lived in was far removed from where a star would ever visit, let alone live. Their questions ran the gamut between stars they hoped I had met, all the way down to the mild temperatures I had enjoyed while living there.

In between answering their questions, I scanned the room subtly and saw the girl I had met the previous day with her brother sitting together eating lunch. Both were watching the group I was eating with intensely, and I smiled at both of them when our eyes met. Bethany frowned slightly at my smile and her brother Matt merely grunted and looked down at the table as he resumed eating his sandwich.

"Don't mind him," Rebecca said quietly, not missing the exchange. "He's got a chip on his shoulder since the school keeps holding him back. He was supposed to graduate with my brother two years ago, but had to repeat tenth and eleventh grade."

"That's what his sister told me yesterday. Are the classes here that hard?" I asked nonchalantly, like it really didn't matter.

"Not really, the teachers are really great. Usually, if you don't get something, they're pretty good about spending extra time helping pull you through," she said, shrugging her shoulders.

My first big shock of the day came once lunch was over. I watched the other students around me grabbing their math and world history books once the desks were back in their rightful places.

"Where are we going?" I asked Rebecca, grabbing my purse and hoodie off the back of my chair.

"We rotate to other classes for math and history," she explained. "We go to Mrs. Glenn's class first for history, and her tenth graders go to Mr. Hanson for math, while his eleventh graders come in here for science with Mr. Graves," she continued.

"That's kind of kooky," I said, not overly crazy about meeting a new teacher just when I had gotten comfortable where I was.

"It's not bad. Both Mrs. Glenn and Mr. Hanson are nice. They decided to rotate us like this five years ago when bussing us to a high school in another town was vetoed. I guess they figured they'd switch us around to give us a rough idea of what regular high schools are like."

"I guess," I said reluctantly, understanding their logic.

"Don't worry, they're cool," Max said, joining me on my other side.

"Sure, sure, that's what they always say before they feed you to a bunch of sharks," I quipped.

Max laughed at my words. "Nah, not sharks, maybe barracudas," he said, grinning widely. "Kidding," he teased, nudging me. "Trust me, it'd be more like feeding you to lambs. Mrs. Glenn is super nice, especially since she and Mr. Hanson hooked up and tied the knot last year."

"Seriously?" I asked, wondering if it was some big school scandal or something.

"Yeah, they started dating right after Mr. Hanson transferred here like two years ago and got married this past summer. It was a beautiful wedding with the loveliest lavender tulips everywhere," Alicia said, sighing like only a girl would when discussing a wedding.

"So you went?" I asked, completely floored that the teachers and students seemed to intermingle.

"Heck yeah we went. They wouldn't have even started dating if it wasn't for us," Clint said in the same somewhat cocky tone I was beginning to associate with him.

"That's crazy, I couldn't imagine a teacher from my old school ever inviting a student anywhere, let alone a wedding," I said as we strolled into our history class as a group.

They laughed at my words as they found their desks, leaving me once again as the odd person out with no place to sit. Mrs. Glenn proved to be as sweet as promised and quickly found me a chair and encouraged me to sit wherever I felt comfortable. I settled back with Rebecca who seemed to have no problem sharing with me.

History class moved along rapidly and soon we were on our way to math. Everyone being so nice helped my nervous anxiety which seemed to be subsiding more and more as the day progressed. I was happy to see that catching up this time around wouldn't be nearly as hard as the last few times had been. We've moved so often that every time I start at a new school, I'm always behind. The teachers are hit and miss. Most of the time they're patient and do what they can to help me catch up, but there are always those that couldn't seem to care less, like it's my fault I don't know what I'm supposed to know. I put in the work though, and usually even manage to get my grades up to B's and C's, which is about the time when Lucinda decides it's time to move on again, and then it's good-bye school for another couple of months.

My new confidence level however, nose-dived not two minutes into the math lesson when the teacher proceeded to write algebraic equations on the board for us to solve.

Moving around so much affected my so-called math skills more than anything, and if I had an arch nemesis, that was it. The past couple of years I'd barely scraped by, taking the most basic math the school would offer. I was fine the simple stuff, but once fractions and algebra were brought into the picture, I broke out in hives.

I sank down in my seat as everyone in the class quickly got to work on the problems written on the board. I pulled out my own notebook and doodled in the margin, giving the illusion that I was busily working through the problems. I tried to will the hands on the clock to move as rapidly as they had in the previous classes. Obviously, it wasn't my day for wishes though, because the minute hand continued its painstakingly slow journey around the oversized dial. Finally giving up on my doodling, I studied the problems on the board, writing them out carefully in my notebook so the page would at least have something on it. I could feel Mr. Hanson's eyes on me, but I kept my nose buried, trying to make sense of the problems that may as well have been written in Chinese. Moving them from the board to my paper didn't help the situation. I stared at the letters A, B and X mingling with numbers, without having a clue how to solve them.

Rebecca, Max and another girl whose name I had forgotten, all finished the problems and I watched as they tore the pages from their notebooks and put them in the basket on the teacher's desk. They went right to work on the homework assignment that was listed on the far corner of the dry erase board. Fifteen minutes later, only six of us were still working on the problems from the board. Not wanting to draw anymore unnecessary attention to myself, I tore my own page with its unanswered questions from my notebook. I slowly made my way to the front of the class with a knot the size of Canada in my stomach, placing my paper upside down in the basket. Mr. Hanson looked at me questioningly before giving me a small smile and I turned, hurrying back to my seat without looking back.

Class ended a few minutes later. I gratefully closed my book and surged to my feet, anxious to flee. My new friends surrounded me as we made our way toward the classroom door.

"Katelyn, can you stay behind for a moment?" Mr. Hanson asked, standing by the door.

"Sure," I answered carelessly for my friends' benefit. Inside I was mortified, knowing I hadn't fooled him. What if he wanted to tell me I didn't belong in the twelfth grade and thought I should be moved down? Then I'd be stuck here with Bethany and her brother Matt, all in a contest to see who could stay in high school the longest.

"I couldn't help noticing you seemed to be struggling with the problems on the board," Mr. Hanson said, sitting casually on the edge of his desk.

"Yeah, sorry, math's not exactly my forte."

"Were the problems just too hard, or do you not get them at all?" he probed.

I hesitated to answer, but he sat silently, waiting for a response.

"I didn't have a clue," I finally answered as students I didn't recognize began to stagger into the room.

"I see," he said.

I kept my eyes glued to him, not daring to see if anyone was following our conversation. He was going to send me to the office and demand I get demoted. I imagined the embarrassment of facing Max and my new friends when I returned to class to gather my things.

"Well, it's actually no surprise," he said, startling me as he hopped off the desk.

"It's not?" I asked confused.

"Not at all. The office passed out copies of the information your mother provided this morning and I see that in the past two years you've attended six schools. How is that possible?"

"Um, we just move around a lot," I answered, puzzled where he was going with this.

"How many schools did you attend before that?" he asked, clearly interested.

"I've lost count. I guess maybe twenty or so since fifth grade," I said, trying to recall all the schools I'd attended.

"Is your father in the military?" he asked, sounding confused.

"No sir. My mom just likes to move," I said, trying to make the situation appear normal.

"That's insanity. How does she expect you to keep up if she keeps moving you around?"

"I always manage," I said, trying to cover for Lucinda.

He looked at me skeptically, obviously not believing me.

"I'm sure you do," he said quietly, studying me intently. I flushed slightly at his focused stare. Fooling the teachers here was already becoming a trial. "Well, it's clear we have our work cut out for us. Do you know how long you'll be here?"

I shrugged my shoulders. "We never know," I said, delving out more information than I normally would have.

"Okay, well, first we need to get a gauge of your math skills. I see you took basic math last year. Have you ever taken any kind of algebra class?" he asked as the noise level in the classroom rose.

"No sir."

"I see. Hmmmm—well, I'm going to send home this assessment so we can get a better idea of exactly where you are," he said, rummaging through his desk drawers. "Here we go. This one should give us a rough idea."

"I'll do it as soon as I get home," I said, relieved he wasn't ready to set me back yet.

"Well, relax and take a little breather, then you can work on it."

"Okay," I said, clutching my books to my chest as I fled from the room before he could change his mind about me.

"Hey, what took so long?" Max asked, startling me.

"What are you doing here?" I asked a little defensively as I tried to slide the assessment in between the pages of my text without him noticing.

"I told Mr. Graves maybe I should check on you, in case you got lost," he said, shooting me a mischievous smile.

"Seriously, and he fell for that line?" I asked, unable to resist laughing. "I'm pretty sure you told me earlier that the school's layout was a piece of cake."

"He doesn't know that," he said, trying to appear innocent.

"Well, I know I'm new, but even I realize our class is only two doors down," I said, still laughing.

"So, what did Hanson want?" He asked, changing the subject.

"He wants me to fill out an assessment," I said sighing, not knowing how much he had heard outside the door. All the honesty at this new school was making me slightly nervous. I had gone three and a half months at my last school without anyone getting a flicker of what my life was like. Now, in less than twenty-four hours, the cutest guy I had ever talked to, knew a whole lot more about me than I liked.

"Hey, I'm sorry. I didn't mean to be nosey. Anyway, it's no big deal. Anyone starting school midway through the year might need some help," Max said, misreading my sigh.

"What makes you think I need help?" I asked cautiously, trying to see exactly what he had overheard.

He looked sincere, returning my gaze earnestly. "Well, if you need any help I could come over and tutor you if you want."

"Um, maybe," I said, knowing without a shadow of a doubt that hell would freeze over before I ever invited him over.

"I see you found her," Mr. Graves said as we entered the room, making it clear Max's ploy hadn't gone unnoticed.

Max laughed and winked at me, making my body tingle. It was one thing to resist his dimpled smile, but the wink was my weakness and he was just downright dangerous.

Flustered by his attention, I accidently bumped into a girl's desk that sat directly in front of Rebecca. "Oops, sorry," I mumbled, picking up her pencil I had knocked to the floor.

I glanced at Rebecca as I sat down and was startled to see that her friendly smile from earlier was absent and had been replaced with a pinched smile that didn't quite reach her eyes.

With a sinking heart, I instantly understood that I had committed some kind of faux pas. Following her gaze, I saw she was watching Max's back wishfully. Unease slowly crept through me as I realized I had been flirting with the guy that my new friend was crushing on. What the heck was I thinking anyway? My plan for this move was to make friends and fit in for the short time I'd figured we'd be here. It was insanity to even consider the idea of starting up a relationship that didn't have a chance of going anywhere.

The last hour of class dragged as I sat next to a now silent Rebecca. Finally after what seemed like an eternity, Mr. Graves dismissed us since the school didn't seem to use a bell system. I slung my purse over my shoulder and gathered my school books together as Rebecca did the same.

"Thanks for all your help today," I said, testing the water.

"No problem, I had fun today," she said, shooting me a regular smile this time.

I let out a pent-up breath, relieved she didn't seem to be holding a grudge. "I did too," I said, speaking the truth. *Except for the latter part of the day,* I couldn't help thinking.

Glancing around, I saw Max was trying to break away from his group of buddies to get over to me. Not wanting to stir the coals, I threw a hurried good-bye at Rebecca and Alicia as I darted out the door before Max could intercept me.

Chapter 4

Kevin met me at the halfway point of the hallway with a huge smile plastered across his face.

"Hey punk, how was your day?" I asked, even though it was written all over his face.

"It was the best first day ever, Katelyn! I already made a friend," he said, proud of himself.

My heart swelled at his words. Making friends was always difficult for him, being quiet and small for his age. His insecurities about his size always made him clam up and only after a few months would he finally begin to emerge from his shell. Usually, this transformation would occur just when Lucinda decided to uproot us again.

"Yay! Good job, pal. I told you this would be a good place," I said, nudging him with my hip as we descended the front steps of the school.

"Yeah right, you weren't saying that yesterday when you found out we'd be in the same school," he joked.

"That's true," I laughed. "But I guess it's not that bad."

"Ugh, there's Mom and Jim," Kevin said, pointing to Lucinda who was parked directly in front of our school. "She could've at least tried to hide the car a little," he added, since we both could hear the car idling loudly by the curb.

I grimaced in agreement at his words. Our string of crappy vehicles had been an embarrassment for me for years, but Kevin had only recently become aware that the rust, bald tires and bad exhaust weren't virtues when you were being dropped off near your peers. I was at least thankful that the rusted hole in the back floorboard wasn't visible from the outside. It may have been cool for the Flintstones to drive a floorless car, but not so much for us.

"Well, let's hurry before Jim does something that'll really embarrass us, like pick his nose or something," I said, shooting a grin at Kevin.

He smiled back. Jim definitely wasn't the brightest stepdad we've had over the years. His obsessive habit of picking at every surface on his body was enough to make us gag. Kevin was only two years old when Lucinda left his dad, and Jim is stepdad number seven since then. She never legally married any of the guys she hooked up with, she just liked to refer to each one as her spouse. I was pretty sure it had something to do with the fact that she had never officially divorced my dad. The only time she played the single mom card was when she was in the welfare office. Then it paid to be single. She was the queen of finding loopholes in the system and played the "woe is me card" perfectly. This time her system-manipulation had paid off, giving us the roof over our heads. Eventually though, she'll get sick of Jim just like she had with all the others and we will have to deal with a huge blowout of a fight. Usually afterwards, she plays up the battered woman role, even though most of the time, she does the majority of the beating. I once saw her bury a pair of scissors in stepdad number four's thigh when he tried to walk past her. When the cops arrived at the scene, she had convinced herself she did it because she feared for her life. The cops took one look at the trashed motel room we were staying in and of course took her word for it. They hauled number four away, and we never saw him again. The motel then, not so graciously, escorted us off the premises after that.

"True dat," Kevin said, using a phrase he had picked up on TV.

The car door groaned loudly in protest as I pried it open with all my strength. I glanced around, hoping the noise had gone unnoticed. My mouth dropped open in shock as I saw Max climbing into the black SUV Kevin had admired that morning.

Max's eyes appraisingly met mine just before I ducked down to climb into the vehicle before Kevin. I tried to analyze his look as Lucinda slowly pulled our noisy Chevy through the rest of the parent loop. He had definitely seen me climb in an old beat-up car, he knew we were on food stamps and lived in a trailer park and yet, by the way he had been looking at me, none of that seemed to matter to him.

I felt my crush on him beginning to grow as we pulled away. We had a long forty-five minute drive to the city, giving me time to think, but unfortunately, time for doubt to creep in also. Was he only being nice because he was under the impression I was easy or something? Why else would he be interested in someone like me when he had girls like Rebecca waiting in the wings.

By the time we finally pulled up to The Salvation Army thrift shop in Bozeman, I had convinced myself that Max and I could never be together. I felt sick, knowing I would have to immediately put a stop to his advances. If living with Lucinda had taught me anything, it was that I didn't want to be like her. I wasn't going to rush into any relationship with a guy.

"You think you'd be happier about getting new stuff," Lucinda said sarcastically as we piled out of the car.

"Oh, I am," I answered quickly, not wanting to stir anything up. "I was just thinking about an assignment I need to do later tonight," I lied.

"What? They gave you homework on your first day? I could've predicted that when we walked onto their prissy-ass campus this morning. Well, I wouldn't knock myself out doing it," she muttered as she flicked her cigarette butt onto the sidewalk, even though there was a receptacle can right by the front door.

"I won't, Mom," I fibbed. Lucinda was not a fan of formal education, and had tried on more than one occasion to get away with the whole homeschooling idea, but Kevin and I always balked at the idea. Thankfully, most of the time when we got into government housing, it was a prerequisite that she enroll us in school.

Kevin and I headed right to the racks of boys' clothing once we entered the building while Lucinda and Jim went to the adult clothing section. I sighed as I watched their retreating backs. The bulk of the thrift store voucher was supposed to go to school clothes for Kevin and me since we had no winter wardrobe to speak of. I could see that I would have to stick to my guns if Kevin and I stood a chance of getting anything.

Thumbing rapidly through the racks, I pulled anything warm that looked to be Kevin's size. I found four pairs of jeans that seemed to be in relatively good shape and sent him off to the dressing area to try them on. All but one pair fit him perfectly. The fourth pair was just slightly baggy, but I added it to our cart anyway, taking what we could get. I added a dozen long-sleeved shirts in an array of colors and patterns to the pile, not even bothering to have him try them on. Even if they were too big, they would have to work since the selection wasn't all that great. The thought of buying used underclothing always gave me the creeps, but I found two pairs of long johns that were his size. Kevin tried to protest when he saw them, but I convinced him they were necessary.

"Okay, now you just need a heavier jacket than your hoodie," I told him after outfitting him fairly well with warm clothes.

"Can I go to the toy section while you find one?" he pleaded.

"No, dopey, you'll need to try it on. Come on, we'll make it fast," I promised him as I spied Lucinda's overflowing buggy across the store.

We hit pay dirt with the coats immediately, finding him a snow jacket that looked practically brand-new.

"Sweet! And it's blue," he crowed happily as I zipped him up in it.

"Perfect," I said, making him turn around so I could make sure the fit was right all the way around.

"Okay, now you can go look at the toys," I told him. He scurried off before the words could leave my mouth.

Smiling, I turned back to the cart to mentally add up the contents. The jeans were pricier than I would have liked at six dollars a pop, but I knew they were a necessity. Thankfully, his shirts and pajamas were only two bucks apiece. His winter parka was the biggest bargain for ten bucks, taking his total up to sixty three dollars. With that number in mind, I headed over to the teen section for myself.

The selection of jeans in my size was decent, and I was surprised they were two bucks cheaper than Kevin's. Long-sleeved shirts were another story, though. I could only find three that would work, and they were twice as expensive as Kevin's. I couldn't really make sense of the store's pricing, but I guess it didn't matter, it is what it is. Giving up on the shirts in frustration, I headed toward the jackets, hoping to find something nice. I found a pretty pink parka and several hooded sweatshirts that were super cheap. The hoodies gave me another idea to look at the selection of regular t-shirts. Finally I scored, finding a dozen shirts to wear under the hoodies, all bargain priced at only a dollar. I also threw a few pairs of long johns into the buggy for myself, including a set that was a pretty light pink and another in lavender. The one place I drew the line was getting a used bra, knowing I could make do for a while with the two I had. Adding up the total for my stuff with Kevin's, I was relieved we were only at one hundred-twenty dollars. I was hopeful Lucinda would stick to her promise and let Kevin get a couple non-clothing items and maybe some books for myself. I pushed my cart to the back of the store where they stocked the books and happily lost track of time, thumbing through their selection. One good thing about thrift stores was that they always had a ton of books and at only a quarter a piece, I soon had a large stack on the floor beside me.

"Katelyn, where's Kevin?" Lucinda asked, suddenly standing over me.

"Over by the toys, why?"

"I was gonna go find him some clothes," she said, sounding motherly for once.

"Oh, I found some for him," I said.

"Oh, thank goodness. I'm ready to leave this store. Did you find any books?"

"Yeah, I picked out twenty. Is that okay? It'll only be five dollars."

"That's fine," she said generously.

"Thanks Mom. My clothes and Kevin's equal one-twenty, with my books, it's one-twenty-five. I know Kevin is looking for a backpack and maybe a toy," I said, trying to give her a rough idea of the money situation.

"That's fine. Mine can't be much over that same amount. We'll probably get a credit back."

I skeptically eyed her buggy, finding her words hard to believe.

"We still need to get blankets and a few towels," I added, wording it carefully so she wouldn't get mad.

"Damn, that's right. Let's go see how much the leeches want for their linens," she said, pushing her buggy toward the bedding section.

"Mom," I chastised, looking around to make sure no one heard her.

"What?" she asked, starting to get aggravated.

Wishing For Someday Soon   Tiffany King

"Nothing, it's just, all of its free to us so..." I let my voice trail off.

"Yeah? But if we didn't have the voucher they'd be sucking us dry. We could practically get this stuff new for the prices they're charging."

I sighed, but kept my mouth closed, not wanting to ruin her good mood.

Going through the rack together, we both found comforters we liked. I talked her into getting one with Star Wars on it for Kevin, even though she thought he was too old for it. I won the battle when I pointed out it was the cheapest one in the lot.

Towels were a bargain too at a dollar apiece and we picked out ten of the largest ones that looked the most durable. Now that we had overflowing carts, Lucinda and I rounded up Kevin and Jim. Kevin hit the jackpot by finding a gallon-sized Ziploc bag filled with superheroes for only two dollars, which made up for the plain-Jane black backpack Lucinda made him get since it was only a dollar.

Jim wanted some fishing gear too, but luckily Lucinda vetoed the idea and sent a sulking Jim off to put his stuff away. We could hear his grumbling as we made our way to the front of the store, but I tuned him out working on the math in my head. With Kevin's purchases, including the toys, all of my stuff and the linens and blankets, we were at a hundred-sixty-three dollars. As long as Lucinda's stuff

71

didn't surpass a hundred-thirty-seven dollars, we would be okay.

Lucinda and Jim headed out to smoke while I handled the purchases.

Keeping an eagle eye on the register tape, I watched as the woman began to scan Lucinda's clothes through. I groaned when I saw several dressy shirts, completely inappropriate for our lifestyle being scanned. Lucinda had an addiction to pretty clothes that she never had the opportunity to wear since she very rarely went out or worked. I grimaced when Lucinda's clothes hit the ninety dollar mark and there was still Jim's stack to go through. I mentally went through my items, wondering what I could put back if we exceeded the amount. My books would be the first that would have to go and that would at least give us an extra five dollars to work with.

The sales clerk finished with Jim's clothing and our total sat at a hundred-fifty-five, nineteen dollars over what we had to spend. I pulled Kevin's stuff out of the buggy first, stacking it carefully as she scanned it through. The linens went next, followed by the jacket I needed and my jeans. By the time she rang my hoodies and long johns through, we were at our limit. She hadn't got to any of my shirts yet, or the couple pairs of sweats I had picked up to sleep in. Not knowing what to do, I continued to let her scan the items through even though I knew we were going over.

"That'll be three hundred forty-four dollars," she said as I handed over our three hundred dollar voucher.

"Um, we went over. I'm sorry, I should have said something sooner," I said mortified, knowing I had caused her extra work.

"Well, let's see what we can do," she said nicely, studying the voucher over her rhinestone spectacles. "Ah, it's a voucher from Thurston House. Well, we can take the taxes off because you get a tax free deduction," she said, hitting a button that took our total down to three hundred twenty-three dollars.

I grabbed the last bag that had my books and sweats in it and started to pull out the contents.

"Now, now, not so quickly. Did you know that Wednesdays are senior days?" she asked. "And judging by the worn-out look on your face, I bet you could use a senior day break," she said with sparkle in her eyes as she hit another button on the register, taking the total down to two hundred ninety-three dollars. "See, much better," she said, handing me a gift certificate for seven dollars.

"Thank you so much," I said, feeling a slight tickle in my throat.

"My pleasure, dearie, now you go home and take care of yourself and your sweet brother," she said, nodding at Kevin who was bouncing around outside.

"I will," I promised, loading our bags into the buggy.

"Did you get a voucher for the credit?" Lucinda asked as I pushed the buggy out the front door.

"Yeah, but it was only seven dollars," I said, shivering in the cold, not bothering to tell her what the kind "leech," as she had referred to the woman earlier, had done for us.

"Shit, I told you they were a bunch of blood suckers," she complained to Jim as they stubbed out there cigarettes.

"Not really," I muttered as I loaded our bags into the car. "We all got a lot of stuff," I continued in an offhand manner.

Lucinda continued to complain as we pulled out of the parking lot, but I tuned her out by reading one of my new books from the bag I had placed on the seat beside me. Her voice faded away as I quickly lost myself in the story. I often speculated that if there was a God, he must have given me the gift of losing myself in a book as a lifeline. When I was reading, it didn't matter that we were all crammed into the car together twenty-four-seven, or that we had skipped several meals. I could immerse myself so completely into a book that everything else became trivial.

My reading was interrupted when Lucinda pulled the car into the parking lot of a laundromat.

I stifled a groan. I knew we needed to wash the clothes, but after the stress of the thrift store, I just wanted to be back at our temporary home. "Can we do it at the laundromat at the trailer park?" I asked hopeful.

"No, it only has two washers. Besides, Jim and I deserve a coffee break while you and Kevin do the laundry," Lucinda said, handing me a stack of crumbled up one-dollar bills. "This is it for cash until Jim can find work," she added.

"Okay, I'll make it stretch," I said, smoothing out the bills as I went to retrieve a cart to transport our clothes into the building.

After I loaded up the clothes and laundry soap we kept in the trunk of the car, Lucinda and Jim pulled out of the lot, promising to return in a few hours.

I sorted the clothes into three large loads to conserve our money while Kevin used the coin machine to turn the dollar bills into quarters. At least the place was empty, so I could use three machines next to each other. It was a pain trying to keep an eye on several washers scattered throughout the facility.

"Okay punk, thanks for your help. How 'bout a snack?"

"Really?" he asked, racing over to the vending machine.

"Pick one and we can split a soda," I added, feeling extravagant.

He gnawed on his lip. "I don't know, Katelyn, I don't want you to get in trouble."

"It's fine, dopey boy. Mom and Jim are off getting coffee, right? Well, this is our treat. We'll just keep it as our secret, okay?"

He nodded. He was smart enough to know I was breaking the rules, but his desire for something to eat outweighed his conscience.

Several minutes later, I finally had to prompt him to make a choice. He was torn between chips and his favorite candy, Peanut M&M's.

"Why don't you get the M&M's since they have peanuts inside, that way it's like you're getting a double treat?"

"Good idea," he said, grinning at me.

I plunked some change into the vending machine for him and headed over to the soda machine to get us a drink.

"Here you go, sis," he said, offering me the open bag of candy as we settled onto the hard resin seats.

"No thanks, kid, I'm not all that hungry."

"Are you sure?" he asked, not quite believing me.

"Positive," I said, trying to block out the smell of his candy so that my stomach wouldn't growl and betray my lie.

Kevin munched happily on his unexpected treat while I read my book until the laundry was ready to be switched around.

A little later, while the laundry was tumbling in the dryers, I gave Kevin a ride in the laundry cart since the facility was still empty of other patrons. He loved it when I would pretend I was going to crash the cart into something, only to jerk the cart to a stop at the last possible moment. The belly laughs that poured from him made me giggle in delight. Moments like this only clarified why I could never leave him.

Our fun came to a close as the clothes began to dry. Lucinda was seriously obsessive compulsive about her clothes getting wrinkled, and only hers mind you, which seemed like an oxymoron considering that the majority of the time we lived in the car. Though I felt the whole idea was ridiculous, I'd taken enough hits over the years to know it had to be done right. So, as each piece of her clothing became dry, Kevin and I would pull it out and shake it vigorously before smoothing it out on the folding table and rolling it like Lucinda preferred. Rolling the clothes before they were packed helped eliminate wrinkles and crease lines and Lucinda had come to appreciate this method.

Kevin and I finished the laundry as the sun was setting outside, making the temperature fall rapidly. While we waited for Jim and Lucinda to return, I made Kevin change out of his thin worn-out jeans into a pair of the long johns and thicker jeans we had purchased earlier. He also grabbed one of his hot-from-the-dryer, long sleeved shirts to put on over his t-shirt.

Lucinda and Jim pulled into the parking lot as I was sliding into one of my new hoodies. The warmth from the dryer engulfed me and chased away the chill that had begun to creep into the badly-insulated laundromat.

I handed over the change and watched Lucinda as she counted out the three remaining bills.

"How many loads did you do?" she asked, causing Kevin to stiffen beside me.

I patted his hand in the dark, reassuring him. "Four," I lied easily, not feeling any guilt. Kevin having something in his empty belly outweighed lies in my book. "The washers were seventy-five cents each, and each load took fifty cents worth of drying," I added before she could ask, accounting for every cent we'd spent.

Chapter 5

The next day of school went much like my first day had gone except I now had my own desk in each of my classes.

As luck would have it, my new desk was located smack dab next to Max's which seriously shook my resolve to ignore his advances. He was as attentive as the day before and I couldn't help but respond to his easy nature as he continued to pepper me with questions.

"How'd your assessment go?" he asked as we headed out of math class later that afternoon.

"Um, I'm not sure. Hanson said he would go over it tonight," I said, trying to sound blasé.

"Well, my offer still stands," He said.

"Thanks, I appreciate it."

"But..."

"No buts, I'm just not sure what I'll need help with," I answered, trying to skate around the real issue.

"No prob. It all comes easy to me."

"Wow, cocky much?" I asked, laughing at his pretend hurt expression.

"Ha-ha. Nah, I'm not sayin I don't have my faults. Don't even think of asking me to make anything in the kitchen, that's a complete disaster."

"Ha, me too," I laughed.

"Great, our future kids will starve," he said, grinning at me.

"Guess that means marriage is out," I joked.

"No way, we'll just hire a cook or order out," he said, finding a solution to a moot point.

"Genius," I said, still bantering as we took our seats back in Mr. Graves's class.

"So, what are your plans this weekend?" he asked just before Mr. Graves could start in on our science experiment.

"Unpacking," I lied, sidestepping what he was really asking.

"The whole weekend?" he persisted.

"Yeah..." I was cut off as Mr. Graves called our attention to the front of the room.

I glanced back at Rebecca to see if she had caught our exchange and saw the resigned look on her face. I was confused on the whole who-was-dating-whom situation. They all seemed so close. Even earlier that day, I was convinced Clint and Alicia were dating until he hit on me during P.E. class. Alicia had been standing right beside me, and I tried to prepare myself for a verbal attack, but she merely laughed when I turned him down.

The rest of the day passed quickly after Mr. Graves paired us up to do the experiment listed on the board. The steps for the experiment were extensive, so my partner Courtney and I spent little time chitchatting as we did the appropriate calculations needed to complete the task. Mr. Graves strolled around the room, stopping at each group to offer pointers or praise.

"Good job, girls," he said, stopping at our table to compliment us.

"Thanks, I did a similar one last year," I said, feeling a little guilty for the step-up I had.

"Excellent, half the battle is remembering what you've learned," he said, patting my shoulder as he strolled away.

"Man, I'm not sure I've ever had a teacher even half as nice as the ones here," I told Courtney as we cleaned up our mess.

"Well, my dad kind of demands it," she said, stowing our beakers in the appropriate place.

"Your dad?" I asked puzzled.

"Yeah, he kind of heads up the school board here, and I've heard he's tough as nails," she said, laughing lightly.

"Wow, that's really cool," I said, feeling a touch envious that her father had taken such an active role in her education.

"It's a pain sometimes. He always knows everythinggggggggg that's going on," she said, dragging out the word.

"I bet," I said giggling.

"So, I was kind of eavesdropping yesterday and heard you telling the others that you've been to a few schools. What's that like?"

I grimaced at her words. "Not fun," I finally answered honestly.

"Really? I'm a little jealous of all the people you've gotten to meet. Everyone here's cool, but sometimes I crave more space. I hate feeling like we're in a fishbowl all the time with everyone always in your business."

"That's true, but I think it's pretty cool how all of you have known each other all your lives," I said, trying to keep the wistful tone out of my voice.

"Yeah, that part's pretty cool, but it still gets pretty cliquey here," she said, looking over at Rebecca and her friends.

I nodded my head, understanding what she was saying. In my last high school of more than three thousand students, we had the standard division of groups. There were the jocks and cheerleaders, who were all nice for the most part, but preferred to hang with each other since their sports kept them so tightly entwined; the band geeks, who you never saw that much because they were always practicing somewhere; the churchgoers, who enjoyed spreading their message and were always trying to recruit you for some church event. The druggies were neither here nor there. They floated through school like they didn't have a care in the world. The worst of all the groups were the really smart kids. Not the pocket-protector-wearing, tape-on-the-glasses nerdy types, I mean the ones on the college track. They had little time for anyone outside of their realm and enjoyed the exclusivity of their group. Then there were the mice as I like to call them, who were the loners or quiet types. Most of the time they preferred to be by themselves, although occasionally they would be brave enough to accept a friend into their lonely existence. The in-betweeners were everyone else and enjoyed the privilege of floating into any group they chose. That's where I fit in. I usually started the first day as a mouse, but would manage to float into whatever group suited me best.

It was evident here in my two short days at Munford that the groups were a little more simplified: those with a lot of money, those with some money, and then the few with very little money. For the most part, the lines blurred between each group and they all seemed to get along pretty well, with the exception of Bethany and her brother. I wondered, since I lived in the same trailer park, if eventually I would be treated similarly to how they were here, but something tells me it has more to do with them personally than some kind of rich or poor class divide.

"So, are you going to the Halloween dance at Alicia's at the end of the month," Courtney asked.

"Um, I'm not sure. She mentioned it yesterday at lunch, but I'm not much of a dancer."

Courtney laughed in response. "None of us really are either. We all just hang out. You know, listen to music, that kind of thing. It's pretty cool since Alicia's parents bought these big, like oversized outdoor heaters. They set it all up in their barn that's been renovated," she said smiling. "You should come."

"Okay, well that sounds more like my kind of thing." I said, returning her smile. "So, if it's not a real dance, how does everyone dress?" I asked, mentally going through my limited wardrobe.

"Well, that's the funny thing," she chuckled. "Everyone still gets dressed up and everything, just for the fun of it, I guess."

"Oh, well, I..."

"Don't worry, I'm sure you have something that'll work," Courtney said, seeing my apprehension.

"Of course," I said, plastering a fake smile across my face.

Any further conversation was cut off as Mr. Graves dismissed us for the day. Grabbing my stuff, I headed out the door.

"Hey, Katelyn, wait up," Max called after me.

I paused for a moment so he could catch up.

"I have to catch the bus," I said in a rush as he joined me.

"Don't worry, Mr. Macon, the bus driver, will wait on you." Max said reassuring me as I walked swiftly down the hall. "Besides, if you ever miss the bus, I can give you a ride," he added.

"I just don't want to worry Kevin," I said, still not slowing down.

"So, anyway, I wanted to ask you if you would go to Alicia's dance with me." He finally asked, keeping pace with me.

"Won't your girlfriend mind?" I asked a little harshly.

He looked taken aback by my tone or maybe it was my question. "Girlfriend?" he asked puzzled.

"Rebecca," I said, watching the play of emotions cross his face.

"Do you really think I'd ask you out if I was seeing someone else?" he asked earnestly, grabbing onto my hand to halt me.

"I don't know. It just seems like there's something there," I answered truthfully.

"We went out a couple times, but I've also gone out with Alicia and Courtney. We've all known each other so long that when we do try dating it never fits right. The only two that seemed to make it work are Brandon and Shirley," he said, naming the other two in their group. "They've been going out almost since she moved here."

"I think the girls may feel differently," I said.

He sighed, raking a hand through his hair. "I know I guess, but I can't force something I don't feel, especially now that I know how it should feel," he said, looking at me meaningfully.

"You don't even know me," I said quietly.

"Then give me the chance to get to know you," he replied sweetly.

I looked down at our hands that were still linked and relished in the warmth his hand was giving mine. "What if you don't like what you find out?" I finally said meeting his eyes, more vulnerable than I've ever felt in my life.

"I don't think that could even be a remote possibility. Will you go with me?" He asked once again.

Finally caving under his charm, I nodded.

A broad smile spread across his face at my nod. He squeezed my hand before he loped off to join his friends down the hall.

I watched his retreating back for a moment before rushing off so I really wouldn't miss the bus.

I mumbled an apology to the bus driver, who, by the way, was a dead-ringer for a mall Santa Claus with his white hair and long beard.

"No problem dear. Your brother Kevin here, told me you would be coming," he answered, winking at Kevin who was sitting in the front row.

"Front row?" I asked, arching my eyebrow at Kevin.

86

"I always sit up front," he said.

"You do?" I asked, preferring the back myself.

"Yeah, no one bothers you up here since the driver can hear everything," he answered knowingly.

My heart pinched at his words. I knew that at some of his old schools he had gotten picked on because of his size and such, but I never realized it went to this extent.

"Well, as long as I'm with you, you have nothing to worry about," I said, swallowing hard.

"I know, but these seats are the coolest anyway," he said, shooting me the grin I loved the most.

"Whatever you say, punk," I said, nudging him with my elbow.

I looked up and saw the driver's eyes on us through the mirror. Our eyes met and he just smiled, acknowledging that he had heard our whole spiel.

I scanned the occupants of the bus and it looked to be mostly fifth or sixth graders and younger, with the exception of Bethany and her brother who were sprawled out in the last two rows of the bus.

I sighed heavily, already dreading my daily commute, even though I had bigger problems to worry about. I had no idea how I was going to ask Lucinda for a dress. I knew our cash was gone, leaving only the seven dollar voucher from the thrift store. I was sure I could find something suitable there, but convincing Lucinda was a whole other story. I would have to phrase it just right and wait for the perfect moment to spring it on her.

The bus driver made two stops before finally stopping in front of Shady Lane. Kevin and I piled out before Bethany, Matt and several younger kids I had seen playing throughout the trailer park over the past couple of days.

A cold gust of air hit us in the face as we made our way down the dirt path toward our trailer.

"So what do think of Mun-crapville?' Bethany asked, catching up to me.

"I like it," I answered honestly.

She looked disappointed at my words. "I guess you would," she muttered condescendingly, slowing her pace to trail behind me.

"What does that mean?" I asked, puzzled by her tone.

"I mean that Max has taken quite a liking to you. It won't last, though. You need money coming out your ass to fit in with them," she said, looking at me knowingly.

"What makes you say that, and besides, why would that matter anyway?" I asked, almost sarcastically.

"I just know from past experience. They all think they're better than trailer park trash like us," she said sadly, all bite leaving her voice as she shuffled off to join her brother.

I pondered her words, climbing the steps to our trailer. Were my new friends really that superficial? Max already knew about the food stamps and the beat-up car, surely, living in a trailer park wouldn't be the straw that broke the camel's back.

The next day dawned with a not-so-pleasant surprise of several inches of frozen snow blanketing the ground, making for a miserable walk to the bus stop.

"This sucks," Kevin grumbled, shivering as he slipped for the twentieth time.

"I know, right," I said, reaching to steady him once again.

"Why is it so slippery? It wasn't like this in Colorado," he complained.

"I don't know, but it's freakin cold. Bet you're glad I forced those long johns on you now?" I said, slinging my arm around his shoulders to help his balance.

"Heck yeah, I'm still cold even with all these clothes on," he said, indicating the bulk that encased his narrow frame.

"At least we know school will be toasty warm," I reminded him.

"True dat, sista," he said, using his gangsta voice.

"Needs work," I said.

The bus rumbled to a stop and we all boarded, sighing with pleasure as the heat of the interior soaked through our cold limbs. By the time we got to school, we were all nicely thawed out and didn't relish the short hike to get to the front door.

"You need a hat," I told Kevin as we raced up the school steps with our heads down, hoping to ward off the chill.

"I know," he said with bright red cheeks.

"Maybe when Jim finds a job, we can ask Mom, okay?" I reassured him.

He nodded before heading off toward his class after a boy his age called his name.

Class seemed to fly by that day. It was obvious from the moment I walked through the door that Max had told everyone about our upcoming date. I flushed uncomfortably as I met Rebecca's eyes. She gave me a small smile, which was a relief. At least that was less one obstacle I needed to obsess over.

Max was as engaging as ever, and I couldn't resist the magnetism between us. I pushed Bethany's claims to the back of my mind. For once in my life, it seemed possible that everything could work out.

Mr. Hanson snagged me at the end of math class to give me the results of my assessment.

"Well, Katelyn, your basic math is dead on. You scored very high in all those categories. Fractions and algebra seem to be your kryptonite," he said, smiling at me.

"No surprise there," I answered, smiling at his Superman reference which would have pleased Kevin immensely. "I just never really remember really learning either one," I admitted.

"Never?" he asked shocked.

"No, sir."

"Hm... Well, now that we have a starting point, we can get you the help you need. Can you stay after school one day a week for extra lesson time?" he inquired.

"Um, I don't think so. I ride the bus."

"Would your mom be willing to pick you up that day?"

"I don't think so," I said trying for indifference, but really just too ashamed to tell him she was too busy applying her makeup and styling her hair to actually leave the trailer to come and get me. "Could I do it during the school day?"

He nodded his head. "How about during lunch twice a week? I have two tutors in mind, so you can take your pick. One is Maxwell Jones, or there's Courtney Weaver."

I smiled. "Well, Max has been hounding me about how great he is at math, so I guess I'll take him up on his offer."

"That's a good choice. Max has a way with numbers. He's taken our school to state each year in the Math Quest competition and placed first in the whole state two years running."

"Wow, seriously?" I said, feeling a bit intimidated.

"Don't worry, he will be an excellent tutor," he said, smiling at me.

"Okay," I said, before heading out the door, only to bump into the object of my unease.

"Hey, I know I have animal appeal, but please control yourself. We are at school after all," Max joked, steadying me with his hands.

"Very funny," I said, regaining my balance, but trying not to think about how right his hands felt on my arms.

"So, you get your wish," I said, taking a step back to put distance between us.

"Oh yeah, what wish is that?" he asked, smiling suggestively at me in a way that made my heart skip a beat.

"To tutor me, you perv," I said, feeling flustered at the way I was reacting to him. I was no novice to dating, but I had never been sucked in so completely by someone I hardly knew.

"Sweet, so you've finally come to your senses."

"Well, I guess if Hanson says I need a tutor you'll have to do," I teased as we entered the room late once again.

"Don't mind me you two. It's not as if I'm trying to teach or anything," Mr. Graves joked as we took our seats.

"I tried to tell her that, Mr. Graves, but she moves like a snail," Max said, shooting me a mischievous grin.

"I'm sorry, Mr. Hanson needed to speak to me," I said, glaring unsuccessfully at Max.

"I know, John told me he would be speaking to you after class," Mr. Graves said, reassuring me. "He didn't say anything about you however, Mr. Jones."

"I had to walk milady back to class," Max said in a deadpan English accent that made the class roar with laughter.

I blushed as he shot a wink my way.

"Oh please," Mr. Graves said, trying to look stern.

I kept my eyes down, trying to control the heat that had crept up my neck. If there was any question about Max's intent before, he just answered it in front of the whole class.

When the day ended, it seemed only natural to wait for Max before I headed out of the classroom.

"Here, I'll take those," he said, plucking the stack of books from my hands.

"Thanks."

"So, can I give you a ride home?"

"Isn't it out of your way?" I asked, trying to find an excuse.

"Nope, I work tonight, so it's exactly on my way."

"Well, I promised Kevin I would ride the bus with him," I said, grasping at straws.

"No problem, he can ride with us," he said, squelching the last of my protests.

"Um, okay."

"Hey, don't worry, I'm a good driver," he said, hearing my reluctance.

"That's not it."

"Then what is it?"

"It's nothing," I answered, trying to dodge the question.

"Katelyn," he said, pulling on my hand so I would look at him. "Why don't you want me to take you home?"

"I don't want you to see where I live," I said, mortified that he had gotten the truth out of me.

"Katelyn, I already know where you live. Have you seen the size of this town? Everyone knows everything. Come on, let's go get Kevin," he said, pulling me down the hallway.

I followed behind, wondering when my life had become an open book. Keeping secrets was my trademark, and within three days of meeting Max, all my secrets were out in the open.

Kevin was over the moon when he found out we weren't riding the bus and practically crowed in delight when he saw Max's SUV.

"Holy moly, this is like something Batman would drive," he said, climbing onto the plush leather seats in the back.

I stifled a groan. "Sorry, Kevin is obsessed with superheroes."

"That's why I picked this one," Max said, looking at Kevin through the rearview mirror.

"Really?" Kevin asked, awestruck.

"Of course, is there anyone cooler than Bruce Wayne?" Max asked, talking Kevin's kind of language.

"Exactly," Kevin said before he launched into a full account of Batman's attributes and why they set him apart from every other superhero.

Max had no problem keeping up with Kevin's mania and made a point to add in his own two cents.

I sank back in my seat and listened to Kevin happily jabber away with the guy that was slowly beginning to weed his way into my heart. I knew none of this could end well. We were on borrowed time and yet I couldn't help but let myself be pulled in.

Kevin piled out of the vehicle as soon as Max pulled up to our trailer.

"Thanks for being so great with him," I said, lingering behind.

"It's easy to do, he's one cool dude."

"Thanks, I think so too."

"You guys seem really close."

"We are. He's all I got," I said honestly.

If Max thought my comment was odd since I obviously had my mom, he let it slide by.

"You sure you can't go out this weekend?" he asked before I could climb out of the SUV.

"What did you have in mind?" I asked, no longer wanting to fight his advances.

He grinned at me. "It's Clint's turn for movie night tomorrow. We were all going to head over there. You game?"

"Sure, I guess. What time?"

"How about sixish? Don't eat before I pick you up, we'll eat there."

"Do I need to bring anything?" I asked nervously, pulling on my lower lip.

His eyes dropped down to my lip, distracting him. It was embarrassing, but the lip pulling was a nervous tick I had that I couldn't seem to shake no matter how hard I tried.

"Just yourself," he finally answered.

"That sounds good," I said, climbing out of the vehicle. "I guess I'll see you tomorrow," I added as the trailer door behind me slammed open.

I closed his door hastily and turned to face Lucinda.

"Who's that?" Lucinda asked, taking a long pull on her cigarette.

"Just a guy from school," I said, walking around her to climb up the stairs. I sighed with relief when I heard Max's vehicle pulling away.

"Pretty snazzy car," Lucinda said, following me into the trailer. "Is he slumming?" she asked meanly.

This was nothing new. Lucinda was all for me dating since she hoped I would prove her right by being as promiscuous as she was. Her joke was to constantly tell me I was bound to wind up barefoot and pregnant. Her words scared me to the core and I had made it my mission to prove her wrong. I cautiously picked who I would date, and

I set all the rules, including my own curfew. If the guy turned out to be a complete toad, my curfew was always unusually early. The same thing applied if he turned out to be an octopus and couldn't control his groping. Lucinda said I was a tease since I had many first dates, but not a whole lot of second dates. What she didn't know was that most guys bored me, they were either too immature, too self-centered or were too hands on.

"I guess," I answered, heading toward my room with her on my heels which filled me with apprehension. Something was off. She seemed almost jittery. "Where's Jim?" I asked.

"Off looking for a job," she grumbled, lighting up a new cigarette.

"That's good," I said in relief. We definitely needed an influx of cash.

"Fine for you to say, you're not cooped up in this stupid trailer all day."

My heart dropped at her words. It was not good for her to be sick of our new place this soon.

"You could see if the grocery store is hiring," I said, grasping at straws, forgetting that Max's dad owned it.

She snorted unattractively, "Why would I do that? We're getting this place free for the next two months, and after that the rent is only three twenty-five a month," she said sarcastically.

"I just thought you might want to get out."

"Well, you thought wrong," she said angrily, completely contradicting her earlier complaint.

I was used to her mood swings, though, and had learned to adjust for them.

"You should try writing. You're always talking about if you had time you would love to write," I said, trying to appease her before the situation got out of hand. "I saw all kinds of used computers at The Salvation Army, maybe you can go get one when Jim gets his first pay check."

All animosity left her face as she considered my words. "That's not a bad idea. I can start making notes now," she said, heading toward her room. "Get me a cup of coffee," she added as an afterthought before I could head off to my room.

Relieved that the bomb had been diffused, I set my book bag on my bed and headed off to the kitchen to get her coffee.

Chapter 6

The next day was a flurry of activity. Between cleaning the trailer and shopping for more groceries, I had little time to dwell on my date that night. I was grateful for the activity since I knew I would have been a basket case by the time Max arrived. By four o'clock, the chores were done and anxiety began to creep in.

I started to doubt my decision to have our first date with his friends. I had seen and read enough movies and books to know how cruel people could be. What if it was all a joke and they had some hidden motive? I could just imagine a bucket of pig's blood being dumped over my head or something else twisted.

My vivid imagination had me near panic by the time I got out of the shower. Using the side of my wrist to wipe the steam off the bathroom mirror, I studied myself critically. "You should cancel," I muttered to my pale reflection.

As much as my reluctance was trying to win, I shook off my anxiety and finished getting ready. I pulled my hair back in my customary neat ponytail. Wearing it down was out of the question since I was forced to leave my heat iron and blow dryer behind when we moved. I didn't have much of a chance to miss them when we were living in the car or the shelter over the past month, but now that we were somewhat established, I felt their absence acutely.

I dressed in one of my new-to-me hoodies that I hadn't worn to school yet and completed the outfit with the nicest jeans I owned.

"You look nice," Kevin said, coming into my room.

"Thanks, punk. What are your plans for tonight?" I said, feeling a twinge of guilt for leaving him.

"I'm going to draw."

"Do you have paper?" I asked, reaching for my book bag.

"Yeah, Ms. Davis gave me some drawing paper when she found out I liked to draw," he said happily.

"Well, that was nice of her."

"She gave me markers and colored pencils too," he added, grinning at me over his windfall.

"Wow, that's great, Kevin," I said, ruffling his hair and making a mental note to thank his teacher the next time I saw her. Getting new stuff was a foreign thing for Kevin and me and any new gift was highly regarded. "Why didn't you tell me last night?"

"You were busy with mom," he said, not needing to say more. Even at nine, he knew to lay low when it looked like things might boil over.

"Well, I expect the best picture ever by the time I get home," I said, giving him a one-armed hug as we left my room.

"How 'bout I make you some dinner," I said, glancing at the clock and then at the door that was closed down at the end of the hall.

"Okay," he said, plopping down on the couch with his art supplies and his favorite program on the TV.

"You want mac & cheese?" I asked, looking in the cabinets for something quick to prepare.

"Yum, that sounds good."

I prepared his dinner while I kept one eye out the window. I wanted to catch Max before he could knock on the door. Keeping him away from Lucinda and Jim as long as I could was the best plan of action I could think of.

Kevin was munching his dinner at the coffee table when Max's SUV rumbled into the dirt space beside our beat-up car.

"I'll be right back," I told Kevin, grabbing my bag and heading outside.

"Hey, I would have come to the door," Max said, coming around the vehicle.

"That's okay, but I was wondering if I could get your cell number in case anything comes up here."

"Sure," he said, opening the passenger door of his vehicle so he could lean over the seat to grab a pen and a piece of paper out of the middle console.

I couldn't help but admire his backside as he leaned over.

"Here you go," he said, abruptly turning around in time to catch my admiring glance.

He smiled brightly, making me blush heavily at being caught.

"Okay, I'll be right back," I stuttered, turning on heel to head back up the stairs, wondering what it was about him that made me lose control.

.

"Here's a number you can reach me at," I told Kevin in a rush as I handed the slip of paper over. "Call me if *anything* happens," I added, making my point clear.

He nodded his head solemnly, knowing without asking what situation would warrant a phone call. Four days of peace was unheard of and a blowup could be only moments away.

I glanced back at him one last time as I bounded down the stairs. I was immensely relieved that the owner had equipped the trailer with a working phone line, there was no such thing as cell phones in our family.

"Everything okay?" Max asked, still standing by the passenger door where I had left him.

"Yeah," I said, looking behind me at the closed door. "Everything's fine," I said, trying to reassure myself more than him. This was not new territory for me, but I always felt like a traitor leaving Kevin behind. Lucinda never took her anger out on him, but I hated that he even had to listen to the battles. By the time he was two, Kevin had been exposed to every curse word imaginable and more violence than anyone should ever have to see.

Max looked concerned, but I smiled at him. "You sure it's okay to go?" he asked.

"Yeah, it's good, let's go have some fun," I answered, allowing him to help me into the SUV.

"You look nice," he said, settling into the driver's seat next to me.

"Thanks, you too," I replied, speaking the truth. The jeans he wore fit him well and had that faded look that came that way when you bought them, as opposed to mine that were faded because they were just worn out. He topped it with a black, long-sleeved thermal shirt under a deep grey hoodie. The casual look served him well, even with his model-like good looks.

"So whose house are we going to again?"

"Clint's. He and I take turns hosting movie nights because we both have big TV's with surround sound and stuff. Plus, like I told you, the closest theater is almost an hour away."

"That's cool," I said, not quite sure a bigger TV was still in the same league as a movie theater.

Max smiled at me in the dim light. "Trust me, once the movie starts, you'll never want to go to a theater again."

"Wow, that's a strong statement."

"How about we bet on it?" He said, grinning mischievously. "If I win, you come to my house next week for my turn at movie night."

"What if I win?" I asked, arching my eyebrow at him.

"Then we take a drive to the city and see a movie at the megaplex there."

I returned his smile, seeing that win or lose, another date was on the horizon.

"What if you decide you don't want to see a movie with me next week?" I teased.

"Not even a possibility," he said, looking scandalized.

"You never know," I laughed. "What if I'm one of those people who laughs at all the inappropriate parts?"

"Then I'll laugh with you, so you don't feel bad," he countered easily.

"What if I like to throw popcorn at all the lame parts?" I said, having a hard time controlling my giggles.

"Then I'll pretend I don't know you," he said without cracking a smile.

"Whatever," I laughed, slapping him on the arm.

"Okay," he busted out laughing. "Maybe I'll just hold your hand to take it out of commission."

The thought of him holding my hand was enough to send butterflies fluttering across my tummy.

"Alright, one more, what if I'm one of those people who likes to talk through the entire movie?" I asked less playfully.

"Then I guess I'll have to distract you so you'll forget about talking," he said huskily, making my heartbeat race out of control.

I wasn't sure how to feel about the direction our banter had taken. Usually, I maintained strict control with every guy I went out with, but Max seemed to have a way of getting my guard down. I was glad when it seemed we had arrived, interrupting the conversation. Max turned off the main road onto a dirt drive, leading to a house about a quarter of a mile in. He maneuvered his oversized SUV around the circular drive before parking it beside a BMW and a Jeep Wrangler I had seen at school.

The drive was paved in the same bricks that covered the exterior of an extravagant house that was by far the biggest I had ever seen. I instantly felt out of place as I took in the wraparound porches on both floors and the intricate mahogany door, inlaid with a stained-glass window that would rival one you might see at a church.

"Holy crow, that's a big house," I said before I could stop myself.

Max chuckled as he climbed out of the vehicle and walked around to my side.

"What are you doing here?" I muttered to myself before Max could open my door.

"Come on, you'll be fine," he said, seeing the anxious look on my face before I could mask it.

I sat frozen, gnawing nervously on my bottom lip and feeling puny in front this mansion of a structure.

"Are you sure?" I finally asked, giving all my trust to him.

"I promise," he said solemnly, gently grabbing onto my hand.

His touch helped calm my nerves somewhat, and I allowed him to pull me from the vehicle.

He held onto my hand firmly as we headed up the three steps to the elegant porch.

I glanced around as Max knocked on the door. The porch was a reader's dream with large padded chairs that begged you to settle in for an all-day reading spree with a good book.

"Dude, what took so long?" Clint complained as he opened the door.

"We're right on time, knucklehead," Max said, sticking out his closed fist so Clint could pound it.

"Hey Katelyn, I'm glad you could make it," Clint said, shifting gears to give me a one-armed hug.

"Thanks for inviting me," I said stiffly, not used to such easy affection.

"Everyone's in the kitchen loading up their plates. Maria hooked us up with a killer taco bar," he said over his shoulder as we followed him and the noise through the house. I couldn't help feeling like Alice when she fell down the rabbit hole as we passed one room after another. Each room was tastefully decorated and looked like it was awaiting a photo shoot for Better Homes and Gardens or some other home magazine.

The noise level increased as we neared the kitchen which opened up to the entire backside of the house. I'd never seen anything like it in person, stainless steel appliances, marble countertops and an oversized fireplace. It had to be any cook's dream kitchen.

"Hey, Katelyn," Rebecca, Alicia and Shirley said in unison, rushing to our side.

I smiled at them, relieved by their warm welcome.

Looking around, I saw a few other students from class, including Courtney and her boyfriend, Chad, who was a junior. Three of the kids I didn't recognize, so I assumed they were also juniors like Chad. Doing a quick head count, I saw there were sixteen of us in all. The kitchen was so large that our group didn't seem nearly as big as it would have under normal circumstances.

"Everybody load up and let's head downstairs for the first movie," Clint said loudly, trying to organize our group.

I moved in line behind Max as everyone made their way through the buffet-style setup. I usually hated loading up a plate of food in front of other people, but it all smelled heavenly and I couldn't resist putting a little of everything on my plate. Max grabbed two cans of soda and stuck them in his jacket pockets while I grabbed napkins and silverware in my free hand.

Max led me through a doorway right off the kitchen that held a staircase leading to a lower level. I followed behind, marveling at the plush carpet that cushioned each step I took. Finally reaching the last step, I nearly laughed out loud when I realized Max had suckered me on our bet. A television almost as tall as our trailer lined the far wall of the dimly lit room. The movie magic continued with two rows of eight leather reclining chairs each. An old-fashioned popcorn machine sat along the back wall along with a soda machine and a cabinet holding every movie candy imaginable.

"I think I've been hustled," I mumbled to Max as we settled into the first row of seats.

"Just stacked the odds in my favor," Max said out of the corner of his mouth before winking at me.

Feeling flustered by his attention, I looked down at my plate as everyone else piled into the room. Clint used one remote to turn on the TV and another to control the lights. Sound came at us from all sides thanks to the several speakers that lined the wall.

"Wow, this is just like a theater," I said as the opening credits flashed across the screen.

"Told ya," Max said, smirking at me knowingly.

"Okay, you win," I conceded.

The rest of the night was a blast as we watched two blockbuster movies I had been dying to see. Before the second movie, Clint made popcorn for everyone and passed out candy. I hadn't had this much fun in a long time and by the time Max pulled up in front of my trailer at the end of the evening, I felt drunkenly happy.

I shivered in the cold as he helped me down out of the vehicle.

"Sheesh, it gets cold here," I complained as I stomped my feet, trying to warm them.

"You get used to it," Max laughed, rubbing his hands vigorously up my arms to help warm me.

"I had a great time tonight," I said facing him.

"So did I," he said, leaning in just as the trailer door burst open behind me.

Max jumped back like he had been scalded. "Hello, Mrs. Richards," he said politely to my mom as she took a long draw on her cigarette.

I backed up from Max and headed for the steps before Lucinda could say anything. "Thanks again," I told Max, using my body to block Lucinda as much as possible.

"Um, okay, I'll see you at school on Monday," Max said, looking at me strangely.

Chapter 7

I was glad I had kept the goodbyes abrupt since I discovered Lucinda was picking for a fight as soon as I closed the trailer door. A pissy mood was to be expected, given the fact she was left to take care of her own needs for one night. She gave me the full verbal assault, calling me every name imaginable until I was finally able to escape and retire to my room. At least the attack wasn't physical. I had once heard someone say that verbal abuse was worse than physical abuse, which is a bunch of crap. I would take Lucinda's verbal rants any day over a beating. After years of being called the worst names possible, I had learned to tune it out and still look appropriately hurt at the same time. Physical attacks on the other hand, came so quick and unexpected that I had no time to prepare myself mentally for them. I knew that anyone looking into my life would wonder why I didn't toughen up and challenge Lucinda. What they couldn't understand is that you can never win with her. If I stood up to Lucinda, she might decide to start going after Kevin, or she might decide to up and leave one day, taking Kevin and leaving him to deal with the repercussions alone.

I put up with all of Lucinda's crap for one reason and that was Kevin.

Lying in bed, I tried to find a feasible solution to being able to see Max while keeping him away from the nonstop drama that was my life. I finally came to the conclusion, after tossing and turning for hours, that I would just keep it casual. That way, if Max decided dating me wasn't worth the baggage I came with, he could back out. Easy peasy, no harm no foul. Satisfied with my resolve, I finally drifted off to sleep.

The next morning I woke late to find the trailer unusually quiet. Creeping out of bed, I discovered that the late night attack had exhausted Lucinda and she and Jim were sleeping in. Kevin and I decided to take advantage of the peace and quiet by spending the day together. The only time we heard from them was when they made demands for food or something to drink.

All day, in the back of my mind, I worried about how Max was handling the abrupt goodbye from the night before. I'm sure he was probably confused over why I didn't introduce him to my family like any normal person would do, but there was nothing normal about my family.

My one goal last night had been to get Lucinda as far away from him as I could.

Enjoying our freedom, Kevin and I hung out in the living room, minus the television, though, since it had been moved to the room down the hall. Kevin was disappointed when he discovered its absence, but he kept his complaints to a minimum. Instead, he worked on another picture that he wouldn't let me peek at while I buried myself in a book. It was by the same author that Mr. Graves was reading to us in class, and I absolutely loved the writing style. The author had an uncanny knack of being able to suck you in, making you feel like you were a part of the story. Since the book was highly suspenseful, I spent the majority of the time anxious for how it was going to end.

Dusk was just beginning to set in when I read the last page of my book.

"How 'bout some dinner?" I asked as Kevin continued to work on his masterpiece.

"Okay," he said, not looking up.

I headed off to the kitchen, tickled by his diligence. I absolutely loathed cooking, but made an effort for Kevin's sake.

"How about spaghetti?" I asked, pulling the jar of Prego sauce out of the cabinet.

"With meat?" he replied.

I held up the package of ground beef I had gotten the day before, making him grin happily.

I was letting the sauce simmer on the stove while the noodles finished up when the only phone in the trailer rang for the first time since we had moved in.

I picked up, expecting it to be a wrong number.

"Hello."

"May I speak to Katelyn?" Max's voice asked, coming across the line.

"This is she," I replied as a smile stretched across my face.

"Hey, it's Max."

"I kind of figured that," I said teasingly. "How did you get this number?" I asked curiously.

"From my iPhone when you used it last night to call home," he said, proud of himself.

"Clever."

"Oh yeah, I'm practically Sherlock Holmes."

"True dat," I said, using Kevin's favorite line.

His laughter filled the phone line.

"Anyhow, I was calling to see if I could give you guys a ride to school tomorrow?" he asked, sounding hopeful.

"Ummm," I said, stalling for time. On the one hand, I wanted to see him and not riding the bus was definitely a perk, but on the other hand, he was making it hard for me to keep our relationship casual. "Isn't it way out of your way?" I asked, trying to throw up a roadblock.

"No, I actually pass your place on my way to school every day."

I mulled over his words as I dumped the water from the spaghetti noodles down the drain.

"Okay," I said, finally conceding.

Max whooped with delight at my words. "Great, I'll pick you guys up at eight fifteen," he said before hanging up.

The dial tone filled my ear and I slowly put the phone back on its cradle. I grimaced at my lack of willpower. I knew I was playing with fire by letting him get so close, but I couldn't help the draw I felt toward him. He was unlike any guy I had ever known.

***

True to his word, Max pulled up into the driveway at eight fifteen on the nose the following morning. Jim had already left for his new job as a day laborer at some construction company, so Max pulled into the space closest to the door.

Kevin and I bounded down the stairs before he could even put the vehicle in park.

"I would've come to the door," Max said as we climbed into the car.

"That's okay, we were ready," I said, glancing back at Kevin to make sure he was buckled in.

The ride to school went fast as Kevin and Max chatted away like long-lost friends. I tuned out most of their conversation once it turned back to superheroes, which became a very popular topic for them the rest of the week.

The daily commuting kept me in a happy bubble, discovering new things about Max every minute we were together.

We also had our math tutoring time twice a week. Staying focused on algebra proved to be a challenge, spending that kind of intimate alone time without our other friends around. I noticed small little habits he had that made him even more endearing. Like the way he would rake his fingers through his hair when he was trying to get a point across, or how he had a dozen different smiles that all kept my heart beating erratically, especially when they were directed solely at me.

"What time should I pick you up tomorrow?" Max asked as we headed toward his car on Friday afternoon with Kevin bringing up the rear.

"Um, five should be okay," I answered, climbing into the vehicle as he held the door open for me. "Lucinda's supposed to take me shopping tomorrow, and it shouldn't take too long to find a dress."

"I wouldn't be so sure of that. Before my sister headed off to college, she could make dress shopping an all-day affair."

"Well, I'm pretty decisive."

"Max, can I play on your iPhone?" Kevin asked as per usual on the drive.

"Actually, buddy, look on the seat beside you, in that case," Max said, pointing to a black leather case on the seat. "It's my iPad. I thought you might like the bigger screen better."

"Sweeeeeeeet," Kevin said, dragging out the word as he turned on the electronic device. For someone without any tech experience, Kevin had become a pro in the short week Max had been chauffeuring us around.

"Katelyn, look how awesome this is," he said, holding it up so I could see the large screen.

"Neato, bud, but make sure you're careful with that. Those things cost a lot."

"I will," he promised as he clicked onto his new favorite game.

"Don't worry," Max said, watching me keep an eye on him. "It's been sitting on my desk untouched for the last six months. It was cool at first, but between my iPhone and laptop, I really don't have much time for it."

"Still, be careful," I told Kevin.

Max grinned at me.

"What?" I asked.

"Sometimes you sound just like an adult."

"Is that a bad thing?" I asked, feeling a slightly paranoid.

"No, it's a good thing. Matter of fact, it's one of my favorite things about you. I like how you never seem to worry about the things girls our age normally harp on."

"Like what?" I asked, smiling at the way he viewed most girls our age.

"Oh you know, dieting, clothes, who likes who, blah-blah-blah."

I laughed at his words. "Maybe I'm not a girl," I joked.

"Oh trust me, you're definitely a girl," he said, shooting me an appraising look.

I felt my cheeks tinge with color at his words and glanced back at Kevin to see if he was paying attention, but to my relief, he was busy dealing with the Angry Birds on the iPad.

"You sure about that?" I asked daringly.

I watched him swallow at my words "Tomorrow night I'll show you how sure I am," he finally answered, looking at my lips.

My heart raced. We had yet to share our first kiss, and it was slowly driving us both insane. Spending each day side by side in class hadn't helped the situation any.

"Thanks for letting me use your iPad," Kevin said as we pulled up to the trailer.

"Why don't you keep it for me this weekend," Max said, reaching back to grab it.

"Really?" Kevin asked before I could intervene.

"I'm not too sure about that," I said.

"Trust me, it's fine," Max said, winking at Kevin.

"Yeah, trust him," Kevin piped in, hugging the treasure to his narrow chest.

"That way he can text us tomorrow night if he needs to get ahold of you," Max said, playing a card he knew I wouldn't be able to resist.

"Fine, but you have to be extra careful with it," I told him, closing the vehicle door.

We both waved at Max as he backed out of the driveway.

"Make sure you hide that from mom," I told him before we headed inside. The last thing we needed was for Lucinda to see it and decide to pawn it for a carton of cigarettes or something.

"I will," he said, stowing it in his backpack.

I checked on Lucinda before heading to my room to get my homework out of the way so it wouldn't be hanging over my head. I found her holed up in her room, busily writing on a notebook.

"Do you need anything?" I asked, poking my head in the room.

"Just a computer," she mumbled, turning the page in her notebook.

"I'm sure you'll find one tomorrow," I said, reminding her of her promise to take me shopping for a dress.

"Yeah yeah," she said, shooing me off like an annoying fly.

I just let the issue drop rather than push any further. When Lucinda got a wild hair to try something new, she would leap in full-force, forgetting about everything else.

Through the years, she had attended every trade school imaginable, always getting right on the verge of completion before deciding the venture wasn't for her. It was the same story with each new place we lived or every guy she hooked up with. She must have found her soul mate at least a dozen times by now. Eventually though, the novelty would wear off, Prince Charming would be toast, and we were hitting the road to another new state that would be the answer to all our dreams—Lucinda's dreams was more like it. All I could hope was that the writing obsession would last and maybe we would stay here for a while.

***

Dress shopping the next day went surprisingly well when I found the perfect dress right off the bat at the thrift store. With the help of Kevin, I was completely buttoned up in a deep rust-colored velvet dress that seemed to accentuate my pale skin rather than wash me out further. It was longer than any dress I had ever worn, sweeping down to the tops of my toes, making me feel like I was in the Victorian era. Long delicate sleeves trimmed in old-fashioned lace slimmed down my arms to end at a point just beyond my wrist. Kevin applauded as I swirled around to show off. Flushing with happiness, I left the dress on and headed toward the shoe section.

I absolutely detested buying used shoes, but knew that my sneakers wouldn't cut it with the dress.

Wishing For Someday Soon

"Katelyn, you look great," Jim said, offering out rare praise when he saw me in the shoe department.

"Thanks," I said.

I critically scanned the size sevens with no real idea what color shoes to get. Seeing multiple pairs that might work, I pulled them off the shelf and lined them up on the floor. I separated any that looked too beat-up or worn, dwindling my stack down to a forth of it where I started.

After twenty minutes of indecision, I was near despair, stressing over which pair to select.

"Get the delicate black ballet slipper ones," Lucinda said, coming up behind me.

"These ones?" I asked, bending down to pick them up and slipping them on my feet.

"Yes, those are perfect," she said, looking satisfied.

"Thanks," I said, smiling at her.

She returned my smile and looked at me affectionately for the first time in months.

"Did you find a computer?" I asked, sensing where the good mood was coming from.

"Yep, an HP desktop. It looks almost brand-new," she crowed.

"Wow, that's great. How much?" I asked casually as I returned the discarded shoes back to the rack.

The price she quoted was definitely going to stretch our budget.

120

"I need ten to cover the difference from the voucher. Is that okay?" I asked, keeping my fingers crossed.

"Sure," she said, still smiling happily.

It was partially my fault for encouraging Lucinda to write, so I felt I really shouldn't complain about them using the majority of our cash to buy a computer, but that didn't help the sickening knot in the pit of my stomach.

On the way home we stopped off at Wal-Mart to pick up cartons of cigarettes for both Lucinda and Jim. I insisted that Kevin needed gloves and a hat, so I shepherded him over to the kids' department to see if they had anything. Not surprisingly, he picked the ones with Batman emblems plastered across them. On our way back to find Jim and Lucinda, we spotted a clearance section of backpacks marked down to three dollars apiece. Finding one with Batman that matched his hat and gloves, I grabbed it up.

"We can at least ask, right?" I said as he studied the backpack longingly.

Lucinda only agreed to let Kevin get his backpack once she was sure they had enough money for their cigarettes. What else was new? In the past, Kevin and I had witnessed Lucinda spend our last three dollars on her cancer sticks instead of getting us something to eat, so we were both well aware of where we ranked in the pecking order.

It came down to our very last cent, but Kevin left the store with the backpack clutched securely in his arms. He grinned the entire way home and I couldn't help reaching over and ruffling his hair. Seeing him happy made me happy.

We arrived home moments before Max pulled into the drive. I grabbed my purse and peeked in on Kevin who was happily playing on Max's iPad.

"Remember to keep that out of sight," I reminded him, dropping a kiss on the top of his head. "You remember how to use the texting app too, right?"

"Yep," he said, not taking his eyes off the screen.

"Okay, see you later, punk."

"Bye, sis," he said, finally looking up.

Max was just about to knock on the door when I pushed it open, making him take a quick step back.

"Oops, sorry," I said, giggling at his quick reflexes.

"No problem, it's only my nose," he pretended to grumble.

"Seriously, I am," I laughed, climbing into his Navigator, anxious to get out of the frigid temperatures that had come out of nowhere. The newscaster on TV had said that it would be too cold to snow which completely confounded me. It just sounded like an oxymoron. As far as I was concerned, if it was snowing, it was cold, so being too cold to even snow seemed crazy.

"How was your day?" Max asked, cranking up the heat as he backed out of our drive.

"Good. I found the perfect dress right away," I said excitedly.

"Wow, that's amazing. You must have radar senses or something to find one that easily. My sister, Trish, would drag us from one shop to the next, for hours, and then settle on one she had seen at the very first store. I personally think she did it to torture me."

"I'm sure," I agreed, not bothering to tell him I only had the option of one store.

Max slowed the SUV, turning down a dirt path two miles from my house. Right on cue, I began nervously tugging on my bottom lip at the thought of meeting his parents.

"You know, it's very distracting when you do that," Max said, putting the vehicle in park between another SUV like his and a dark blue pickup truck.

"What is?" I asked confused, turning to look at him.

"Tugging at your lip like that," he said, reaching over to caress my bottom lip with the pad of his thumb.

His hand slid to the side of my face and I sighed uncontrollably, running my tongue over my lip where his thumb had previously been. His eyes darkened as he watched. He slid a hand behind my neck, anchoring me in place.

I shivered in anticipation as he leaned toward me with clear intentions.

Suddenly, headlights flickered behind us, breaking the spell.

"Well crap," Max said, dropping his hand reluctantly. "The others are here," he continued, clearly disappointed.

I sighed, having a hard time curbing my own disappointment.

Max smiled. "Later for sure," he said, climbing out of the vehicle.

He pulled my door open and reached up to help me down, pulling me in for a quick hug. "Is it later yet?" he asked huskily, voicing my own desire.

"I wish," I said, pulling back as our friends joined us.

Together, we headed toward his house. I kept my gawking to a minimum this time, though I was pretty awestruck at the entire structure. Where Clint's house had a formal Victorian feel to it, Max's looked like a large ski resort lodge I had seen pictures of in the past. Multiple hand-carved wooden rockers lined the porch that overlooked a small frozen pond off to the right of the house.

The interior was warm and inviting with large rooms filled with honey-colored wooden furniture and plush leather couches and chairs. Fireplaces burned throughout the house keeping the wind that howled outside at bay.

We entered the kitchen as a group and I saw an attractive couple cooking dinner together with obvious affection.

"Mom, Dad, this is Katelyn," Max said, introducing me.

"Katelyn, this is my mom, Karen, and my dad, Maxwell Sr.," he said.

"Katelyn, it's a pleasure to meet you," Karen said, reaching in to give me a quick hug. The delicate smell of the perfume she wore enveloped me. I held myself rigid at her touch, unaccustomed to another female hugging me. By the time I thought to return the hug, I found myself in a crushing hug by Maxwell Sr.

"Something smells good," Max said, moving around the large island to peek into the stock pot sitting atop the stove.

"Sweet, chili and cornbread," he said, sneaking a look into the oven.

"Hey, out of there," Karen said, taking a swipe at him with a checkered oven, mitt.

"Aww, come on Mom," he said, dancing out of the line of fire before placing a quick affectionate kiss on her cheek.

"Ladies first," she admonished him, shooting me a warm smile.

"Yeah, ladies first," Alicia piped in, moving to grab a deep ceramic bowl off the counter.

The rest of us followed suit and filed past Max's dad as he ladled oversized spoonfuls into each of our bowls while Karen pulled the cornbread from the oven.

The enticing aroma of the spices wafted through the air as I sprinkled shredded cheese over the top of my chili.

Max and I were the last two of our large group to leave the kitchen. He led me down the hallway toward a large room bustling with chatter and good spirits. I sighed with pleasure, seeing it was my kind of room. Several loveseats and recliners were scattered about, along with the largest bean bag chairs I had ever seen, that easily would sit two people.

"These are great," I said, sinking into one of them while Max held our bowls.

"I know, right?" he said, handing both bowls to me so he could join me. "My mom found them online last year and ordered like eight of them."

"Nice," I said appreciatively.

Karen came in and passed out chunks of homemade cornbread once we were all settled in while Max's dad handed out sodas. They took the time to talk to everyone and I could tell all my friends genuinely liked them.

"Your parents are great," I whispered to Max after the movie had been on for a while.

"I guess they'll do," he said, trying to sound nonchalant. "Okay, they're pretty cool," he finally admitted. "Just don't spread it around that I like to hang with my parents," he added, shooting me a wink.

"I don't know, what's it worth to you?" I teased.

"Hmm, I'll have to think about that," he said, arching an eyebrow at me suggestively.

I swallowed hard and couldn't stop my eyes from drifting to his lips.

"You need to stop looking at me like that," he whispered in my ear.

"Why?"

"Because, I don't want the first time we kiss to be in front of my bonehead friends."

"Ah, I see," I said, grinning at him as I gently licked my lip.

"Grrr," he growled, surging to his feet before he could act on my dare.

"Who's done with their bowls?" he asked, pausing the movie.

Laughing at his frustrated tone, I stood up to help him gather the dishes. I followed him down the hall, still chuckling slightly. Karen was in the kitchen cleaning up when we walked in. I joined her at the sink and started rinsing out the bowls.

"Katelyn, I have this. You go watch your movie and have fun with your friends."

"Are you sure?" I asked dubiously, looking at the stack of dishes. I couldn't remember the last time Lucinda had washed a dish, let alone insist that I have fun. I felt a knot form in my throat as I got a glimpse into how it worked in a real family with an equal amount of give and take.

"Of course dear, go have fun," she said, giving my hand a gentle squeeze.

I was lost in thought as Max and I headed back to our friends, so it took me a moment to comprehend when he veered off into an empty room.

Taking in my surroundings, I looked at him puzzled.

Without saying anything, he pulled me into his arms. Finally understanding the detour, I smiled, looking up into his eyes as he ran his hands up my arms, making me shiver.

"I've wanted to do this since I first laid eyes on you two weeks ago," he said, bringing me closer to him.

"Really?" I asked breathlessly, dragging my lower lip between my teeth.

Max groaned, running his hand up to the side of my face so he could run his thumb over my lip once more. "I can't tell you what that does to me when you do that," he said, dragging in a ragged breath.

"Show me," I whispered, more daring than I had ever been before.

Needing no further encouragement, he crushed his lips to mine. My knees turned to putty as he anchored me more firmly to him. His lips were as soft they looked and I couldn't resist touching them with the tip of my tongue, making him groan. Misreading his groan, I retracted my tongue, sealing my lips.

"Uh-uh, open them please," he whispered against my closed lips.

I parted them slightly, giving him the access we both wanted. Time lost all meaning as our mouths became one. Finally, after what could have been mere moments or eternity for all I knew, he finally pulled back, reluctantly.

"We need to go back," he said, still breathing heavily as he rested his forehead against mine.

I nodded, trying not to stare at his lips that were still within reach. His eyes darkened with need as he saw my stare.

"You're driving me crazy," he said, pressing his lips to mine for a quick searing kiss that made my head spin.

"Is that a bad thing?" I asked as he reached for my hand.

"No way, that's a good thing," he said, pulling me snugly against the side of his body as we joined the others.

"Hey, what took so long?" Clint complained. "Dude, you dog," he added, seeing my flushed look and kiss-swollen lips.

"Shut it," Max said, chucking a pillow at him.

Clint plucked the pillow out of the air before it could hit him and threw it back at Max with precision.

Alicia and Shirley giggled as my cheeks brightened with color.

"Let's get back to the movie," Max said after throwing the pillow back at Clint.

Alicia dimmed the lights as Max and I settled back on our bean bag chair.

My eyes met Rebecca's before the lights dimmed, and I felt awful for the pained look she tried to disguise.

I sighed unhappily as the movie came back on.

"What?" Max asked, draping an arm across my shoulder.

"Rebecca," I whispered back simply.

"I know, but trust me, it was never like this with her," he said quietly in my ear.

I nodded. With so few kids at one school, someone was bound to get hurt as couples switched around. At least at a larger high school, you could move on and wouldn't necessarily have to see your crush with someone new so frequently.

"Don't worry about it. I'm sure she's happy for us," he stated, trying to make me feel better.

I snorted at his words. "I doubt that," I said, smiling at how oblivious guys could be at times.

"Well, it was worth a shot," he said, shooting me a half smile.

"Whatever helps you sleep at night," I teased quietly.

All further talk was put on hold while we watched the movie. Max kept his arm around me the entire time. Occasionally he would slide his hand up my arm and toy with my hair lightly, twirling it around his finger. His touch was distracting, and half the movie slid by in a mindless blur as I counted down the seconds until we would be alone again.

"Thank God," Max said when the movie ended after an action-packed sequence.

I was relieved that I wasn't the only one that had been suffering.

Karen and Maxwell were reading in the living room in front of the fireplace as we all filed past. They stood up to say their goodbyes, giving everyone hugs as we left.

"You come see us again soon, okay, Katelyn?" Maxwell said, giving me another bear hug.

"Well, she can't if you crush the life out of her," Karen teased him as she gave me a much more delicate hug. "But you must come back soon," she said, smiling at me warmly.

"I will," I said, touched by their easy acceptance of me.

We called out goodbyes to our crew as we all piled into separate vehicles.

"Well, that was torture," Max said, cranking the heat.

"What was?" I asked with false innocence.

"Sitting that close to you for two hours after the kiss. It was all I could do not to haul you off for a repeat," he growled, not buying my innocence.

"Well, I'm glad it wasn't just me," I said with more honesty than I normally exhibited.

We drove silently for a short time until Max abruptly turned down a narrow dirt road before throwing the car into park.

I looked at him questioningly.

"When I kiss you good night, I don't want to be interrupted," he said, undoing his seatbelt.

He leaned in, settling his lips on mine again. Heat flared through me as he gently cupped my face.

After a moment, he slowly pulled back. "Is this okay?" he asked, gazing into my eyes.

My heart clinched as I considered his words. How had something that was supposed to be casual turn serious so quickly? I pulled away and sat heavily back against the seat. Goodbyes had always been painful, but I also had never gotten this close to anyone before. We had never stayed anywhere longer than six or seven months before Lucinda decided she was ready to move on. No matter how hopeful I was that she would change, it would be naïve to think this time would be any different.

"Hey, what did I say?" he asked, concern coloring his voice.

I shook my head, not trusting myself to speak.

Max tugged on my arm, "Katelyn, tell me why you're so upset," He pleaded.

I took a moment to search for the right words before answering him. "It wasn't supposed to get this serious," I finally whispered.

"What do you mean?"

"I knew if I dated you I needed to keep it casual. I can't get into a serious relationship."

"Why not?" He demanded.

"Because, we're on borrowed time here, Max. Do you know how many times I've moved in the last ten years?" I asked

He shook his head.

"Neither do I, I lost count after twenty."

His eyes opened wide in disbelief.

"It's my mom. She's always searching for something that never seems to be there," I said, trying to offer up an explanation.

"Maybe she found it this time," he said hopefully.

I shook my head miserably. "I don't think what she's looking for even exists," I said.

"We'll cross that bridge when we get to it, but Katelyn, there was no way we were ever going to be casual," he said, dropping a soft kiss on my lips before gently trailing his lips across my cheek. "Trust me, okay?"

I nodded, seeing no other way. Hearts would be broken, but I set us on this path and there was no turning back.

Chapter 8

Max dropped me off in front of our trailer after promising to call me the next day. I floated up the stairs, still feeling the kisses he had left on my lips. I peeked in on Kevin and took a moment to pull his comforter up around him. I tucked him in snuggly, shivering in the cold that had settled throughout the trailer. I closed his door quietly before heading to my own room. I could see a light through the cracks in Lucinda and Jim's door, but was too exhausted to check in with them.

I drifted off to sleep, almost the moment I hit the pillow with images of Max filling my head. The pictures turned to vivid dreams of being locked in his arms while he softly stroked my hair.

My dream world was shocked back into reality by a blow to the side of the head and someone yelling at me. "Katelyn, are you deaf or just stupid? I've been calling your name for twenty minutes!" Lucinda yelled, taking another swipe at me. She struck me in the corner off my right eye, making it tear up immediately. Trying to shake off the confusion, I scooted far back on my bed, trying to get out of reach.

"I'm sorry. I guess I was out," I said, trying to apologize. "What did you need?"

"I needed my goddamn ashtray emptied!" she yelled. "But since you're a selfish bitch, you decided to sneak in here without taking care of your responsibilities!"

"I'll do it now," I said, attempting to stand up, only to be pushed roughly back.

"Don't do me any favors, I wouldn't want to interrupt your beauty sleep!" she said sarcastically, stomping down the hallway.

I tried to regain my senses as I cradled my throbbing head in my hands. It was nothing new for Lucinda to wake me up to dump an ashtray or fetch a cup of coffee. Ordinarily, I was a light sleeper and could hear her yelling, but this was the first time I had ever slept through, which explained Lucinda's rage. She absolutely loathed being ignored.

I could hear her slamming cabinets in the kitchen and cringed, knowing it was going to be a long night.

"What's wrong?" Jim stumbled out, asking her sleepily.

"Nothing!" she yelled. "I'm just trying to get my ideas on the computer and meanwhile, everyone in this goddamn trailer sleeps like the dead. You with your god-awful snoring that makes concentrating impossible, and Katelyn in her room, blatantly ignoring me. It's a wonder anything gets done around here," she said, slamming another cabinet.

I sat on the edge of my bed, wondering what the right move would be. When Lucinda was this far gone it was hard to read what she wanted. Jim must have reached the same conclusion since I could hear him retreating down the hall like a chicken shit.

"That's it, go back to bed!" Lucinda shrieked from the kitchen.

I stood on spaghetti legs, still feeling the effects of the last blow. Once I felt steady, I left my room and walked quietly down the hall.

She was standing at the counter smoking a cigarette as she roughly washed the few dishes in the sink with one hand.

"Mom, I got that," I said, staying a safe distance away. "I'll make you a cup of coffee too," I said, trying to pacify her.

She whirled around, glaring at me and I braced myself for what might happen next.

"Fine," she finally said, sick of the few dishes she had already washed.

She stomped past me and I breathed a sigh of relief, glad I had made the right choice to get up.

I dumped the ashtray that started the entire ruckus and put a cup of water in the microwave to boil. I could hear Lucinda's and Jim's muffled voices as I approached the bedroom door to return the ashtray. Jim was taking advantage of the opening I had created and was feeding her the words she needed to hear. I stood there for a moment, listening as I was painted as the villain. *Jim was such a chump, and he wondered why Kevin and I had never warmed up to him,* I thought to myself as I knocked on the door.

They were both sitting with their backs against the wall smoking when I walked in. Lucinda's new computer sat on a piece of plywood on the mattress in front of her.

I handed over the ashtray silently and headed back to the kitchen as the microwave dinged. I stirred in instant coffee, creamer and sugar, just the way she liked it.

Once Lucinda's coffee was in her hands, I finished up the kitchen before heading to my room with an ice pack in hand.

My bed was not empty when I walked in and I wasn't surprised. Kevin was curled up in a small ball, pressed against the wall. His eyes were open wide as I came in with the ice pack.

"It's okay, bud," I said, climbing into bed beside him. I placed the ice pack to my blazing eye and nearly groaned in agony from the cold against my tender skin. I momentarily looked away, knowing it would only upset Kevin further.

"I heard her calling. I should have come in to wake you up," he said, grief stricken.

"Hey, this is never your fault. You got me?" I asked, reaching over to wipe a stray tear off his cheek.

"I kept-t-t thinking-g-g any minute-e-e you would get up," he choked out, sobbing quietly.

I placed the ice pack on top of the dresser next to me and pulled him into my arms.

"This is not your fault," I said fiercely, hating Lucinda for doing this to us. Kevin's sensitivity was only compounded by her fits of rage.

Kevin continued to sob for several moments as I rubbed his back to comfort him. Finally, his sobs turned to half-hiccups as he sniffled and dried his eyes against my shirt.

"Don't worry, it's almost like a tissue," I teased lightly, earning a watery smile.

"Katelyn, you won't ever leave me behind with her, right?"

"No, buddy. I won't ever leave you alone. How could I? We're waiting for our someday soon right?" I asked gently.

"Yep, someday soon it'll just be the two of us," he agreed.

I nodded my head. I hadn't figured out the logistics, but someday, when I was legal, Kevin and I would leave Lucinda behind.

"Where will we live?" Kevin asked yawning, playing a favorite game of his.

"Somewhere cold," I said for the first time ever. My standard answer had always been someplace warm, but a certain dimpled hunk had me thinking the cold had a certain appeal.

Kevin looked surprised at my answer, but moved on to the next question. "And we'll never be hungry again?"

"Nope, our cabinets and fridge will always be filled to the brim."

"And we'll never move again?" he said sleepily as his eyes drifted closed.

"Nope, we'll never move ever again," I whispered to him.

I watched him lying there asleep. No matter how I felt about Max, Kevin would always come first.

***

The next morning, my face was still on fire from Lucinda's midnight freak out. I winced trying to open my right eye, but to no avail. I sat up quickly in a panic and rushed to the bathroom to inspect the damage. I groaned when I saw my eye resting at half-mast since the skin surrounding it was swollen and comprised of colors ranging from dark navy blue to black. I reached up tentatively to touch the skin and cringed as the pain rocketed throughout my face. This was not my first black eye, but it had been a long time since Lucinda had left a mark where someone could see it. The last time it happened a neighbor had reported it, and we moved the following day. How would I explain this at school on Monday? I ran through several feasible excuses, but came up empty. I looked like I had gotten into a fist fight and lost.

I spent the day icing my eye, hoping the bruising would miraculously disappear. Lucinda was remorseful about her actions and tried several times to engage me in conversation. Under ordinary circumstances, I would have responded and made her feel better about her actions, but the stress of going to school the next day made it harder to forgive her this time. Kevin spent the majority of the day glued to my side, watching me warily. He had seen me suffer Lucinda's wrath multiple times over the years, but usually the marks were hidden by my clothes.

After her attempts with me failed, Lucinda turned her attention to Kevin. She tried to bribe him from my side by offering to let him watch his favorite television program with her in her room. Kevin mumbled some excuse and remained stoically by my side. Lucinda finally stomped down the hall, cursing something about our selfish behavior.

Kevin looked at me worriedly as her door slammed, making the entire trailer shake.

"It's okay, pal, she's fine," I said, reaching over to grab his hand to reassure him. "Why don't we go to my room, we can snuggle, and I'll read you some more from the Harry Potter book you got from school."

"Really?" he asked, bouncing up and down on the couch.

I laughed. "Yeah, really," I said, enthralled over his enthusiasm for the book his teacher had lent him.

We spent the rest of the afternoon and evening lost in the world the author had created. "That was the best book ever," Kevin said as I turned the last page.

"It was really good," I agreed. "If your teacher has the second one, bring it home and we'll read that one too," I said, ruffling his hair as he climbed off my bed. "Night, punk."

"Night, Katelyn, I love you."

"I love ya too." I said, shooting him a smile.

My smile turned to a grimace once he was out of sight. The pain from my eye had given me a ferocious headache several hours ago. I didn't have the heart to send him away, so I tried to ignore the throbbing pain as best I could. I changed into my pj's and hit the potty one last time before bed and was disgusted to see my eye looked as angry as it had when I first checked it that morning.

The next morning, I woke to a frigid room. I pulled my clothes on under the blankets, dreading the moment I would have to leave the little bit of warmth my bed offered. Finally no longer able to prolong it, I climbed from my bed so I could wake Kevin and get him ready before Max arrived to take us to school.

Max pulled up just as Kevin and I were shrugging into our heavy jackets. We cautiously walked across the frozen ground, slipping and sliding the entire way. I kept my head down, trying to prolong Max seeing my eye.

Kevin handed Max his iPad as I buckled my seatbelt, keeping my face averted.

"Did you get to play some games, bud?"

"Yeah, I'm the king of Angry Birds now," Kevin bragged.

"I bet," Max said. "How are you?" he asked in a husky voice, turning his attention to me.

"Fine," I said, finally looking at him.

He sucked in a gasp as he took in my eye. "What the hell happened?" He asked, reaching over to gently touch the swollen skin.

"I tripped and hit it on my dresser," I said, hoping the excuse sounded feasible.

Max opened his mouth to say something, but looked back at Kevin who was eyeing us anxiously.

He clamped his mouth closed and drove the rest of the way to school in silence. I could feel the rage radiating from him as he drove. I turned and looked out the window, trying to fight back tears. I was confused by his anger and wondered if he was mad at me for my injury. By the time we pulled into the school parking lot, I yearned to tell Max just to take me home, no longer keen on the idea of facing the other students if this was the reaction I would get. I reached over to open my door, but Max stopped me by gently grasping my hand.

"Kevin, why don't you head to class, I need to ask your sister a question about a homework assignment," Max lied believably.

"Okay, bye, Katelyn."

"Bye bud," I said in a voice thick with unshed tears.

"What happened?" Max asked once Kevin closed the door.

I started to repeat my lie, but I could see he knew the truth.

"My mom," I said simply, watching Kevin's retreating backside.

"Why?" he asked, trying to get a handle on what my crime had been.

"I slept through her calling me."

"What the hell could she have possibly needed that would warrant this?"

"To empty her ashtray," I whispered, ashamed that he now knew all my secrets.

"She beat the shit out of you because you didn't empty her ashtray?" he asked incredulously, gripping the steering wheel so hard his knuckles turned white.

"She only hit me twice," I said, trying to defend her half-heartedly.

"Because you wouldn't empty her ashtray," he repeated disgustedly.

I couldn't blame his disgust. We were white trash. The marks on my face were a glaring reminder of how different the world I lived in was to the one he lived in.

"Yeah," I said looking down, wishing I was anywhere else. "Um, I'm sure this changes things for us, so we don't have to go to the dance together," I said, reaching for the door handle.

"Katelyn, what are you talking about?" he asked, grabbing onto my arm to once again stall my departure.

Anger welled up in me. "Look at me. Do you really want to date someone like me? I'm giving you an out!" I said in a rush as the anger that had briefly filled me dissipated, leaving despair in its place.

"Katelyn, I don't want an out," he said quietly, cupping my face so I was forced to look at him.

"You don't?" I asked in a voice shaky with emotion.

"No," he said, leaning in to brush a kiss across my lips. "But she can't do this to you," he said after our lips parted.

"There's nothing we can do," I said miserably.

"Yes, there is. I'm going to have my parents report her," he said with conviction.

My blood froze at his words. "You can't," I said earnestly, grabbing onto his hand.

"Katelyn, you don't have to fear her. By the time she finds out, they'll have a new place for you to live."

"Yes, but without Kevin! You can't report her because they will separate Kevin and me," I said forcibly, trying to get him to understand.

"You don't know that," he said, sounding uncertain.

"I do," I said in a flat voice. "You don't know how it works, you've never seen it. I have. I've met plenty of kids over the years that were placed in foster homes, and in almost every case they were separated from their families. Plus, I'm too old. I'll just wind up in some state facility."

"You don't know that," he repeated in a defeated tone.

"Trust me, they would," I said softly. "Look, I'm just waiting until I'm legally an adult. I have less than one year to go and then I can take Kevin with me."

"So you expect me to turn a blind eye and let her do this to you?" Max said in a loud voice, clearly frustrated at the hopelessness of the situation.

"If you want to be with me, then yes, I need you to turn a blind eye."

Max dropped his head into his hands.

"I'm sorry," I said, feeling sick that my home life was causing so much havoc.

"How often?" he asked.

I knew what he was asking. "Not that often."

"How often?" He repeated, looking at me.

"A couple times a month, sometimes more."

"I want to kill her," he said, reaching over to drag me into his arms.

I sighed, as he kissed me gently. He pulled back slightly, but kept me firmly locked in his arms. "I'm not sure if I'll be able to handle it if she does this again," he said, lightly pressing his mouth to the tender skin of my eye.

"You have to," I said, pulling back so he could see I was serious.

"Katelyn, it rips my heart out to think of anyone hurting you, let alone your own mother."

My heart swelled at his words. The fact that we had only known each other a few weeks seemed insignificant. He knew my every secret and his acceptance of my life had created a bond that I had never shared with another person. I pulled him close and rested my lips on his.

"We better get to class," I finally said, pulling back.

"We could skip," he said, enticing me with his sexy voice.

"Hmm, that could be dangerous," I said, confused at the emotions he was able to evoke in me.

"Only if we do it right," he said huskily, nipping on my bottom lip gently.

My pulse raced, sending liquid fire coursing through me as his teeth pulled gently on my lip.

"Um, class," I said, finally finding the will to pull out of his arms.

He chuckled and released me. "Okay, class it is."

We walked through the quiet hallway toward our class. Before I could turn the knob, Max turned me to face him and eyed my injury critically. "If she does this again, it won't go unpunished. You got me?" he said.

I opened my mouth to argue.

He shook his head to halt my words. "Look, Katelyn, as long as we're together it's my job to make sure no one harms you, including your mom. I'll let this time pass, but it kills me."

I mulled over his words as he pulled the door open, but any retort was halted when every eye in the room swiveled around at our entrance.

"Max, this is getting a bit ridiculous...." Mr. Graves started to say until he took in my swollen eye.

"Katelyn, are you okay?" he asked, stepping in between Max and me.

"Yeah, I tripped at home," I said, embarrassed at the attention I was getting.

"Tripped?" he asked, looking at Max who merely shrugged his shoulders.

"Um, yeah, I tripped in my room," I said.

"Did you ice it?" Mr. Graves asked.

I nodded. "Most of the day," I said.

"Hmm, maybe your mom needs to take you to the doctor to make sure nothing is broken."

"I'm sure it's fine," I said, trying to imagine telling Lucinda she needed to take me to the doctor. I nearly laughed out loud at the thought.

"Are you sure?" he asked, still not looking convinced.

"Positive," I said, glaring at Max for leaving me hanging.

He smiled at me and I could see he had been expecting this kind of reaction. I swallowed a groan. I was going to have to be extra careful not to set Lucinda off. It was becoming quite clear that it wouldn't be as easy to hide things from the administration at this school like I had been doing for years at other schools.

Chapter 9

The rest of the week passed by relatively drama-free, with the exception of Max studying me critically each time I climbed into his SUV anyway. By Wednesday, unease had crept in and I could tell Max meant his threat. He would not hesitate to turn Lucinda in. We discussed it endlessly throughout the week and I tried to get him to see my side, but he was convinced that if we were taken away, a judge would keep Kevin and me together. I knew it was highly unlikely, but Max remained optimistic.

Scared of giving Max the incentive he needed, I catered to Lucinda's every whim throughout the week. She drank up my attention, creating relative harmony throughout the trailer. By the time Max picked me up for the Halloween dance, I was confident with my ability to keep the peace.

Max knocked on the door at precisely six p.m. on Saturday evening. His eyes brightened when he saw me.

"You look beautiful," he said as he helped me into the vehicle.

"Thanks, even with this?" I asked, pointing to the somewhat faded black eye I was still sporting.

"Well, I'd prefer that you weren't someone's punching bag, but it doesn't take away from how nice you look," he said, looking at me appraisingly. "I like this too," he added, twirling a small lock of hair that had escaped my French braid.

"Thanks," I said shyly. "Lucinda was in a good mood so she fixed it for me," I added, trying to come up with something to say.

His face took on a pinched look at my words and he dropped his hand.

I grimaced at my mistake. Max hated it when I mentioned Lucinda since he found out she liked to take her frustration out on me. "You look pretty snazzy too," I said, trying to change the subject.

He took my hint and smiled at me. "In this old thing?" he asked, indicating the tailored black suit that fit him to a tee.

"Old, huh? I'm sure." I said, raising my eyebrows.

He laughed. "After the countless fittings my mom made me suffer through, believe me, I feel like I know this suit better than my own skin."

"Well, kudos to your mom because it looks quite yummy on you," I said brazenly.

"Yummy? You think I look yummy?" he asked suggestively, placing a warm hand on my knee.

"Well, it's the first word that comes to mind," I laughed, blushing slightly as I looked down at the fingers massaging my leg.

My gaze left his hand when I felt the vehicle abruptly turn off the road.

"Are we here?" I asked confused as he pulled the vehicle into a narrow opening that looked like it had been notched out of the forest as an afterthought.

Max unbuckled his seatbelt and turned to face me. "Yummy?" he asked again, making me giggle when I realized why he had pulled over.

"Um, you could say that," I said just before his lips claimed mine. I shivered in anticipation as he deepened the kiss and explored my mouth with abandon.

"Give me your tongue," he begged against my slightly parted lips.

I succumbed to his demands, giving myself to him as he moaned against my lips. He released my seatbelt and dragged me across his lap in one fluid movement without ever breaking the contact our lips shared. I ran my hands up under his suit jacket, feeling the soft skin of his neck under my fingers as I anchored him more firmly against me.

"You are so beautiful," he whispered, pulling back slightly to gaze at me hungrily.

"You're just biased because your choices have been limited here. In a school of a couple thousand kids I'd be lost in the crowd," I said, not used to compliments.

"It could have ten thousand students and I'd still think you were the most beautiful," he said before crushing his lips once more on mine.

I was the one to moan this time as his tongue met mine. I felt his hand on my ribcage, slowly caressing me through the velvety material of the dress. I shifted closer, yearning for his touch like none other. He understood my unspoken plea and adjusted me so I was straddling his lap, bringing us together intimately although we had layers of material between us. His hand continued slowly up my side until it rested just below where I wanted it to be.

"Max, we should go," I finally said, dragging my lips from his. He nodded, but shifted slightly to bring us even closer.

I fought back a groan, trying to control my exaggerated breathing.

"You're killing me," he said, planting one last kiss on my lips before deftly moving me off his lap.

My senses slowly returned, and I was mortified at how out of control I had allowed the situation to get. I acted like Lucinda would have. I felt color creeping up my cheeks as I thought of how close I had come to letting him do whatever he wanted. Had Lucinda been right in all the years that she had been telling me I was just like her? Was I really no better than she was? Giving up my virginity in the front seat of a vehicle with a guy I had only known a couple weeks would have definitely painted me that way.

"Katelyn, are you okay?" Max asked as I studied my hands, mortified.

I remained silent as I struggled with the inner turmoil boiling through me.

"Katelyn?" he said again, more insistent this time.

"I've just never acted like that," I finally muttered, thankful the interior of the vehicle was too dark for him to see my face clearly.

"Katelyn, neither have I," he said, taking my hand into his. "I know things got a little intense there, but we can slow things down."

"I just always said I'd wait," I said too quietly for him to hear clearly.

"What?" he asked, rubbing the inside of my wrist with the pad of his thumb.

"I said I always planned to wait. I don't want to turn out like my mom."

"Katelyn, you're nothing like your mom," he said forcibly.

I remained silent, knowing he was wrong on this point. Our out of control breathing and fogged up windows were all the proof I needed.

"So, we'll be careful not to let things go so far next time," Max finally said, trying to ease my mind.

I gave a shaky laugh. "Like never being alone?" I said.

Max barked out a laugh. "Well, that might help for a while," he said, pulling my hand up so he could kiss the sensitive skin of my wrist.

"Um, just so you know, that so doesn't help the situation," I said, giggling breathlessly.

"Slow then, we can do this," he muttered to himself as he slowly backed the vehicle back up onto the main road.

"Slow," I repeated, looking at him dubiously.

"Hey, you just wait, I'll become the king of slow," he said, noting my doubt. "You might want to fix your hair, though," he added, turning down a graveled driveway.

"Oh no, what did you do?" I complained, looking at the disheveled mess my hair had become. I had been so lost in the moment, I was unaware he had obviously sunk his hands through my hair sometime during his assault on my lips.

"Guess you'll just have to wear it down," he said winking, implying he had done it purposely.

"You did this on purpose?" I asked.

"I'd rather see you wear your hair without 'her' help."

I sighed, not needing to ask who he was talking about. I felt conflicting emotions over Max's obvious distaste for Lucinda. His protectiveness over me was unlike anything I had ever experienced from anyone, but his dislike for Lucinda was a little unsettling. For all her faults, she was still my mom, and she and Kevin were the only family I had.

Max came around to open my door as I was running my fingers through my now wavy hair.

"Ugh, it's a mess," I complained, studying my reflection in the mirror.

"A mess?" he asked incredulously. "Are you looking at the same thing I am? You look great."

"Are you sure?" I asked, still unsure as I smoothed out my dress.

"Absolutely," he answered, tucking me in under the crook of his arm so I was firmly anchored to his side.

The party was in full gear by the time we approached the oversized barn where it was being held.

"This is amazing," I said, taking in the hundreds of orange twinkling lights that had been draped over bales of hay that lined the walkway.

"Yeah, Alicia's parents love Halloween," he said, chuckling as he pointed out an old-fashioned looking cemetery off to the side of the barn.

"I guess so," I said, admiring the endless rows of uniquely carved jack-o-lanterns that bordered the outside of the rustic building.

Max pulled the large door open, and we both stepped into the surprisingly warm building. The inside was decorated just as elaborately as the outside with sconce lighting fixtures on each pillar, holding flickering bulbs made to look like candlelight. Fake cobwebs and spiders covered the rafters, and fog machines created the illusion that we were in some creepy haunted house somewhere.

"This is incredible," I said, trying to take in all the decorations at once.

He laughed. "Well, it should be. I know my mom and Alicia's mom have been working on it for months," he said, talking loudly so I could hear him over the loud music being pumped out of speakers spread throughout the massive space. The music stopped midway through his statement, making everyone suddenly focus on our arrival.

Looking down, I brushed at the skirt of my dress, wondering if I had missed a stain or a tear. Seeing nothing, I looked at Max who shrugged his shoulders, equally puzzled. I patted my hair uncomfortably, wondering if they suspected we had been making out since my hair was now down, although there was no way they could know it was braided originally.

Max grabbed my hand as we approached our friends who slowly began to talk again, recovering from whatever had triggered their silence.

"You look nice," Rebecca said, coming over to give me a brief hug.

"Thanks," I said, still feeling uncomfortable.

Rebecca's greeting seemed to break the ice as a new song started and the chatter once again rose loudly throughout the space.

Max kept my hand firmly wrapped in his, obviously still puzzled over the strange reception we had gotten.

I pushed my unease to the side, deciding to enjoy the luxury of being around Max. Glancing around the space, I saw Max's mom and another lady I didn't recognize refilling snacks on a long makeshift table that was resting on two giant wooden barrels. My eyes moved on, taking in the small dance floor that was empty as everyone stood around talking. I had been to a few dances over the years and was used to seeing the dance floors overcrowded as the entire student body bumped and grinded against each other. Since I had no rhythm, I usually avoided the dance floor like the plague, but I allowed Max to pull me to the empty floor when a slow song began to play. He looped his arms around my waist, interlocking his fingers together so I was pulled snugly against his chest.

"Hmm, this is nice," I muttered as I rested my head against his heart.

"Yeah, I could definitely get used to this," he said, pulling me more snugly against him.

I sighed with pleasure. Taking things slow would be a chore considering being in his arms felt so right.

"I think I should use the ladies' room," I finally said, pulling away reluctantly when the slow song ended and a faster one began.

"Okay, it's inside the house. Do you want me to walk you in?" he asked as Clint called his name across the room.

"Nah, I got it. You go join your friends."

I pulled the heavy barn door open, stepping into the chilly night air. I immediately began to shiver, missing the warmth of the space I had just left. Hurrying up the path, I entered the house without bothering to knock. The interior of the house had a classic feel to it and I instantly felt out of place, passing expensive antiques as I hunted for a bathroom. Coming up empty after passing several doorways, I sighed in frustration. I heard voices coming from the back of the house and went searching for help before my bladder got the best of me. I paused outside the large swinging doors as I heard my name mentioned, recognizing Max's mom's voice.

"She seems like a sweetheart," I heard her say. I smiled at her words, pleased that she seemed to like me.

"And she's quite pretty," a voice I didn't recognize said. "But I almost died when I saw her wearing the same dress Alicia wore last year. We had it specially, made so I know it's the same one. The poor dear must have gotten it from the thrift store we donated it to when we did that big spring cleaning last year. Thank God all our kids have the couth not to mention it."

Mortified by her words, I looked down at the dress I was wearing and began to feel sick at the ramifications of what she said. No wonder everyone looked at me like I was a leper when we walked in. They all knew I was wearing a used dress. I couldn't help wondering if that's what Clint had wanted to tell Max so badly. I slowly started to back away from the door until their words once again stopped me in my tracks.

"Well, it's only to be expected. As sweet as Katelyn is, her mother is some piece of work," Max's mom continued.

"What do you mean?" the other voice asked, their enjoyment for gossip obvious.

"Well, she tried to buy cigarettes with her food stamp card a couple days ago. When Patty informed her it wasn't allowed, she went ballistic. Patty tried to explain that it was all computerized and that the transaction wouldn't be approved anyway. She caused such a ruckus that Maxwell, who happened to be there, had to step in. He took her to the side to explain the situation, and if you can believe it, she tried hitting on him."

"Oh my God, you're not serious?" the other voice said incredulously.

"I kid you not. I guess she thought she would be able to charm the cigarettes out of him."

"And her daughter is dating your son?" the voice I was slowly beginning to hate asked, making her point clear.

"Well, we had our reservations at first, especially after this incident, but when we tried to talk to Max, he wouldn't hear any of it. He seems to have an unnatural hate for her mom and told us in no uncertain terms that Katelyn is nothing like her. We're going to trust his judgment, but this is one time that I'm hoping the apple does fall far from the tree, because if she's like her mother she could have a hidden motive."

"You think she would try to trap Max?" The voice asked.

Shaking with rage, I slowly backed away from the door, wanting nothing more than to get out of there. Just like always, Lucinda was ruining everything and taking me with her. I fled the house, not even bothering to confront Max. I couldn't believe his mom thought I would try to trap him. I had so much more to worry about than trying to trick some guy into getting me pregnant. Her words ran through my head over as I hiked along the road. I would never consider tricking Max, but the possibility of getting pregnant wasn't as farfetched as it seemed before our heavy make out session in his vehicle earlier. Who knows how far it would have gone if he wouldn't have stopped?

I walked the long two miles home, feeling like I'd been sucker punched. I had no idea how I had let things get so out of control. This is exactly why I kept my personal life a secret. By the time I neared the entrance of the trailer park, I was shivering uncontrollably. The pain in my heart made the cold seem insignificant. I willingly embraced it, knowing it was a small price to pay for my actions. I was so lost in my self-punishment, I didn't notice the vehicle until it was almost on top of me.

Screeching to a stop, Max jumped out of the vehicle looking frantic.

"Katelyn, what the hell is going on? You leave to go to the bathroom and never come back. Why did you leave?" he asked, grabbing onto my shoulders to halt me. "What happened?" he demanded, taking in my ashen face.

"I can't see you anymore," I said, between my chattering teeth.

"What? Why? Did someone say something to you? So what if you're wearing a slightly-used dress," he said, struggling to fix the situation.

My heart sunk at his words. So they had filled him in.

"I g-gues-s they c-couldn't wait-t-t to tell you-u," I said as the chattering made me shake uncontrollably.

"It was Clint. He was just being an asshole. The others don't care and neither do I," he said, trying to pull me into his arms, but I held myself back.

"Katelyn, let's talk about this in the car, you're freezing."

"I'm-m almos-st home," I stuttered.

"We have to talk about this," he said, trying to coax me into the vehicle.

No longer resisting, I finally allowed him to lead me to the Navigator, knowing what I needed to do. The situation had gotten out of control and only a clean break would fix it. The warmth of the vehicle was almost painful as it slowly worked its way through my frozen limbs. After several quiet moments, I finally started talking.

"We can't see each other anymore," I finally said, meeting his eyes.

"Why?" he asked, looking like he had been punched in the gut.

"Because we're no good for each other," I said, louder than I intended. "You're just too far from the world I live in," I said calmly, trying to get him to understand.

"Katelyn, do you think I care that you're poor? Being poor doesn't change who you are."

"That's not true. Being poor changes everything. You have no idea what I've seen or the places I've lived."

"Katelyn, so you think I'm some kind of superficial jerk?" he insisted, pounding the steering wheel in frustration.

"Then why do you guys dislike Bethany and her brother so much, if being poor isn't important?"

"I dislike Matt because he was a complete dick to my sister a couple years ago. He wouldn't take no for an answer when he tried to ask her out. He wound up roughing her up, but she wouldn't let my parents press charges. Bethany wound up getting involved, calling my sister all kinds of names, saying she'd led Matt on. It was a big mess and some of the bitter feelings are still there. Matt made my sister's last year at Munford hell," he explained. "But none of that has anything to do with us."

I remained silent, fighting the urge to give in. His pleading tone made it so easy to believe that we could persevere through our differences. Then I recalled the embarrassing words I had heard while I lurked behind the door at Alicia's house. Within days everyone was sure to know about Lucinda. Would Max feel differently once he heard all those sordid details?

"It just won't work," I finally said, swallowing back the knot that had painfully formed in my throat.

"Katelyn, please," he pleaded.

I climbed out of the vehicle, trying to keep my resolve as I focused on reaching my trailer before I caved to his pleading tone.

"Katelyn, life isn't supposed to be this hard," he said, stopping me in my tracks as I was reaching for the door handle.

"It is for me," I said, swiping away a hot tear that had escaped my overflowing eyes.

I stepped into the trailer, walking past Lucinda who studied my ashen face critically. I slid my bedroom door closed firmly behind me, yearning to weep, but all my tears had run out years ago. I hastily dragged the dress that had started it all over my head, barely noticing as several long strands of my hair became caught in the buttons. I pulled my sweats and favorite hoodie on before climbing blindly into my bed. I curled up in a ball, tucking my pillow up to my chest, willing the pain to leave me in peace.

I had spent a lifetime saying goodbye to people I had come to care about, but none of those separations felt as acutely painful as this one.

I had been right all along. Someone was bound to get hurt.

Chapter 10

Sunday passed in a haze for me. My eyes were swollen from my sleepless night, making it obvious to everyone that something had happened at the dance. Lucinda spent the majority of the morning trying to pry it out of me, but all I would tell her was that Max and I had broken up. No stranger to heartbreak herself, Lucinda was all too happy bemoaning the faults of the opposite sex. Jim tried to stick up for all guys everywhere, but one death glare from Lucinda had him retreating to their room for the remainder of the day. Ordinarily, I would have chafed at Lucinda's solicitous behavior, but I welcomed her mindless babble since it kept my mind off the image of Max and his hurt expression.

Kevin was at a loss over my quiet demeanor and spent the day trying to get me to smile. Part of me knew I needed to snap out of my funk for his sake, but a stronger part of me continued to be held down by tentacles of despair. I fluctuated between anticipation of at least being able to see Max the next day and the dread of knowing I would be facing those who had judged me harshly because of a clothing item.

Lucinda offered to let me skip school the next day, and I went to bed knowing I had that option.

Fate took over the next morning when I woke with a fever. My walk home in the frigid late October temperatures had not gone without consequences. My head felt like it was in a vice, my throat felt like I had swallowed razor blades, and my chest felt like it would explode with each cough. In other words, I felt like crap.

"No school for you?" Kevin asked sullenly from my doorway.

"No, I'm sorry bud. I feel like crap."

"No Max, either?" He asked plaintively.

The disappointment in his eyes made my other aches and pains feel insignificant. By breaking up with Max, I had stripped Kevin of a role model he could look up to.

"I'm sorry, Kevin," I said in a quiet voice.

"That's okay, sis," he said, seeing my distress. "I just hate riding the bus by myself."

"I know, tomorrow I'll be better. I promise," I said, holding up a pinky so we could pinky swear.

"Okay, get better," he said resisting as I dragged him in for a quick hug.

"Ugh, you're germy," he giggled as he backed up.

"I'll give you germy," I mocked, acting like I was going to grab him.

"Ick," he shrieked, racing down the hallway, giggling like a loon the entire time.

I laid my pounding head back on the pillow, smiling for the first time in two days. Somewhere in my own misery, I had forgotten the true reason why I broke it off with Max. It was my job to protect Kevin at all costs, which meant that our home life had to be kept from others, no matter how good their intentions were.

My sickness kept me in bed the entire day as I tried unsuccessfully to sleep away my aches and pains. I couldn't shake the fever though, making it impossible to get comfortable enough to get any decent rest. Lucinda lacked real maternal instincts, so staying hydrated and medicated meant I had to fend for myself. When Kevin came home later in the day, I faintly heard Lucinda discouraging him from visiting me. I resented her interference, but knew it was for the best to keep away from me while I was so sick.

Much to Kevin's dismay, I still wasn't feeling better by the next day or the one after that. Bethany showed up on Wednesday with a stack of schoolwork I had missed.

"Wow, you look like shit," she said, standing in my room uncomfortably.

"Gee, thanks," I replied sarcastically.

"We all thought you were faking," she said in her own tactless way.

"We?" I asked, dismayed that my worst fears were being confirmed.

"Yeah, I heard you made quite the splash at Alicia's elite Halloween party," she added spitefully.

My stomach dropped. "Well, thanks for bringing my work," I said, hoping she would take the hint and leave me to my misery.

"No prob," she said, sinking onto my bed.

"Well, I feel like crap," I said, not having to fake the cough that rumbled through me.

"Ugh, you look it too," she said, picking at a loose string on my blanket, avoiding my eyes.

"Did you need anything else?" I asked, trying to get to the root of her visit.

"I was just thinking, since you struck out with the Pops maybe we could hang out sometime."

"Pops?" I asked.

"Yeah, you know, the popular peeps, the rich kids, the 'we're better than you' crowd."

"Oh I get it, sure I guess," I said, feeling both sorry for her and repulsed at the same time as she dug dirt out from under her fingernails, dropping it on my bed.

"Um, but could you not do that on my bed?" I asked, looking at her hands.

"Sure," she said, brushing off her cruddy remnants. "Are you going back to school tomorrow?"

"I think so. I can't afford to miss anymore," I said, feeling panicked at falling even further behind in math.

"Okay, I'll meet you at the bus stop," she said, tromping out of my room in her heavy boots.

"So, you'll be on the bus with me tomorrow," Kevin asked from my doorway.

"Sharpening up on those spy skills?" I asked, raising an eyebrow at him.

"Didn't need to. She talks really loud," he said, making a production of acting like he was cleaning out his ear.

I laughed. "True dat."

"She smells kind of bad too," he said, wrinkling his nose as he stepped in my room.

"I'm sure we've smelled that bad before too," I reprimanded him lightly.

"Hey, no way. Even when we live in the car, you're always clean, and so am I," he said, defending himself.

I couldn't argue with him. I had always worked hard to make sure Kevin and I always looked as presentable as possible. Lucinda had used us countless times to get donations from churches by parading us in front of the sympathetic hearts there. The key was to look poor, but still clean at the same time. It's weird how people judge you. You can't cross the line of just being down on your luck, where they would help you, to being a dirty scum-bum, where they wanted nothing to do with you. Looking poor was never hard to do in our worn-out, discolored clothes, but keeping clean had always been a challenge when you lived in a car.

"Hmm, well, it's not our place to judge. Besides, we've seen worse. Remember Stinky Steve at the last shelter?"

Kevin pretended to gag, making me smile at his antics.

"Oh yeah, Stinky Steve was the grossest ever, with those disgusting, smelly overalls that looked like he..."

"Peed in them," we both said laughing at the same time. "His hair was the worst though. I bet it's been like fifteen years since a bottle of shampoo's touched that head," I added.

"It would run away screaming if it did get that close," Kevin said giggling as he pretended to run away.

"Okay okay," I laughed, holding my side. "Let me rest so I can go to school with you tomorrow."

I rested back against my pillow, feeling slightly winded from my laugh-fest with Kevin.

"Katelyn, can you take care of your brother tonight? I'm exhausted from catering to you the last few days," Lucinda said, sliding my door open.

"Sure Mom," I said sitting up, not bothering to point out that the only thing she had done over the past two days was take care of herself. I was actually surprised she had made it this long. Normally, Lucinda always "coincidentally" managed to get sick whenever anyone else in the family did. And she expected, or rather, demanded to be catered to.

I spent the remainder of the evening fixing Kevin's dinner and straightening up the trailer that had gotten trashed during my two days of convalescence. Actually, I wasn't bothered too much. Emptying and cleaning ashtrays and washing used coffee mugs took my mind off what I would be facing the next day. I was confident Max would try to talk to me, and I had no real idea what I wanted to say to him. Different scenarios ran through my head as I wiped the last of the ashes off the coffee table where someone had neglected to use an ashtray. There was one idea I was considering, which wasn't the best, but the opportunity had presented itself.

The next morning I woke up exhausted from both my cleaning regimen the night before and staying up too late to complete the majority of my missed assignments from school. The only thing I struggled with was the math, but used the examples from the textbook and slowly felt like I was finally getting it.

Bethany and her brother, Matt, met us at the bus stop and I put my plan into gear by questioning them on things they liked to do. Matt never really answered, choosing instead to just watch me warily out of the corner of my eye. Bethany, on the other hand, responded like a flower in the sun. I felt bad about my initial judgments of her after gleaning a wealth of information over the bus ride to school. She lived with only her brother and father since her mother had abandoned them several years back when

Bethany's dad wouldn't give up his love of drinking. I could tell by the way Matt tensed up next to me while she was talking that this was the root of his problems. I felt his pain. God knows I've dealt with enough of Lucinda's addictions over the years. Of course, her issues went a whole lot deeper than just a love of cigarettes and stupid men.

I walked into school with my new tentative friends and felt Alicia's and Rebecca's stares as we passed them near the front office. My eyes remained firmly planted on the sunny yellow walls as we continued toward the classroom. Bethany, oblivious to the inner turmoil I was feeling, continued to chatter on as she tried to cram a lifetime of information into one conversation. One thing I didn't like was the sharp edge of her tone whenever she mentioned the school or our fellow students. Being prejudice obviously ran both ways. In all the conversations I had with the Pops, as Bethany called them, I never once heard them talk about her or Matt with the same animosity she had for them. I stifled a sigh. I hope this course of action didn't turn out to be a huge mistake.

Max was already at his desk when we entered the room. He had his body angled toward my desk and I sensed an ambush. I couldn't help drinking in the sight of him as I approached Mr. Graves.

"Katelyn, are you feeling better?" Mr. Graves asked concerned.

"I'm getting there," I said in a near whisper since my voice kept going in and out annoyingly.

"You sound awful," he said, still looking concerned.

"I think this is the tail end of it," I said, trying to sound hopeful. "Anyway, I was wondering if I can move my desk over near Bethany, if you don't mind."

His face lit up at my words. "That would be excellent. I think she could use a friend."

I nodded my head, agreeing with him.

"Clint and Shawn, do me a favor and move Katelyn's desk over here," he said, pointing to the empty spot on the other side of Bethany.

I noticed he didn't ask Max to help move my desk, judging by the glowering expression on his face, I could see why. I averted my eyes and tried to tune out the whispering I could hear throughout the room. I had drawn the line, and I could feel the shift in the room. I looked at Rebecca to see if she was gloating over Max being free again, but was surprised that she was studying me with what looked like puzzlement and sympathy.

Bethany continued to chatter away once I was settled and acted possessive of me when anyone passed our desks. I nodded my head at the appropriate parts of the conversation and blamed my sore throat for my uncommunicative responses.

I ate lunch with Bethany and Matt that day and for the rest of November. Eventually, the whispers about me stopped, and several of the other students I hadn't had a chance to get to know before became friendlier. Bethany remained possessive of me and would often interrupt conversations if she thought they might lead to other friendships. I didn't resent her attitude since she had unknowingly helped me out.

As winter approached, the days grew shorter and colder. I knew our days in Four Corners were numbered judging by Lucinda's clamorous complaining. Part of me was actually anxious for the move to happen so I wouldn't have to see Max each and every day. Still, the other side of me was filled with deep despair at the thought of never seeing him again. Being in a small school had become both the blessing and curse I thought it would be. It was torture being around Max in every class because I wanted so badly to run to his arms and feel the gentle beating of his heart against me. In the beginning he would stare at me across the room for hours on end. I learned to discipline myself to focus on anywhere but where he sat, and eventually he stopped looking all together. I mourned the loss of his glances more than I could have imagined, throwing myself wholeheartedly into my schoolwork. I had asked Mr. Hanson if Courtney could tutor me in math once I broke it off with Max. She wasn't quite as strong as Max at the problems, but she also didn't distract me like he used to. She and I gradually became friends through the tutoring sessions since Bethany wasn't around. It was more of a superficial friendship on my part since I once again had my walls erected to protect my personal life. I appreciated her easygoing nature though, and wished that I could have gotten to know her better.

As December approached, Kevin became ecstatic when Jim and Lucinda began to get into the holidays like never before. We even arrived home from school one mid-December day to see our very first Christmas tree standing in the corner of the trailer, surrounded by presents.

"What's this?" I asked, completely floored.

"Jim's been getting a lot of extra bonuses at work, so we figured we'd have fun this year. Why, do you have a problem with that?" she asked, sounding annoyed.

"No, it's just we never have before," I said, not bothering to point out all the Christmases and birthdays we had gone without.

"Well, obviously if I could have, I would have," Lucinda said, clearly aggravated with me.

"I know, Mom, I think it's great," I replied, trying to appease her.

"I just don't know about you sometimes, Katelyn. You can be such a bitch."

"I know, Mom, I'm sorry," I said truthfully. I knew Lucinda hated to have her faults pointed out to her.

I headed to my room before the issue escalated, kicking myself the entire time for saying anything in the first place. I could still hear her grumbling about my selfishness as I closed my bedroom door.

The next day we arrived home to see that the presents had multiplied from the day before. Of course, most of them were for Lucinda, but I was pleased to see that Kevin had his fair share too. My pile was the smallest, but that was to be expected since I had picked a fight the day before. Kevin was over the moon when he saw his gifts and would spend hours each afternoon just staring at the pile.

The pile of Christmas presents continued to grow with each passing day as if Lucinda was trying to prove something. As excited as I was at the thought of having our first ever normal Christmas, I began to worry about where all the extra money was coming from. Lucinda didn't work, and I knew that Jim wasn't making very much money as a day laborer. Of course, questioning Lucinda would mean opening up a can of worms I just didn't want to deal with.

The week before Christmas break was supposed to start, Kevin and I came home to a distraught Lucinda.

"What happened?" I asked, closing the door behind us as Lucinda sobbed on the couch.

"Jim-m-m is in-n-n jai-l-l," she said in between her hiccupping sobs.

"Kevin, go to your room," I said.

"Why?" I asked Lucinda once I heard Kevin's door close.

"Because-e-e he-e-e was stealing-g-g copper wiring from his job."

"Are you kidding me?" I asked incredulously.

"Don't you judge him," Lucinda said as her sobs cutoff abruptly.

"Don't judge him?" I asked, feeling the anger rise inside me. "What was he thinking? How are we going to pay the bills if he's in jail?" I added, pointing out the obvious.

"He wanted to give your selfish ass a nice Christmas," she said, rising to her feet.

"Bullshit, he was just being greedy!" I said, completely disgusted at the situation.

"What did you say, you little shit?" Lucinda snarled, enraged with all grief gone from her face. She struck me in the chest before I could defend myself. I dropped to my knees with the wind knocked out of me. Her next blow was with the coffee cup that had been sitting empty on the table. She swung back and hit me across the side of my head, making the room spin out of control as blinding pain gripped my skull. I curled up in a ball, trying to protect myself from her rage that burned out of control, showering me with one blow after another. When her hands began to fall feebly, she resorted to kicking me as her anger reached a climax. Time lost all meaning as I let my mind float away, becoming numb to the beating I was taking. I willed myself to find my happy place, which had changed over the years to suit my age. For a long time it centered on Kevin and me being free from this madness, but recently it had changed to include Max. His image was never hard for me to remember and I allowed myself to sink into his arms as the trailer and Lucinda faded away.

I woke sometime later, unaware of how much time had passed. A deathly pale Kevin was holding my hand, crying silently when I finally opened my eyes.

"Where's Lucinda?" I asked groggily.

"She left a while ago. I was so scared, I couldn't wake you up," he said.

"You couldn't?" I asked, sitting up. My stomach dropped at my movements. I lurched to my feet and rushed to the bathroom as my stomach released its contents. I rested my head weakly against the side of the sink. I groaned as a sharp stabbing pain shot through from the top of my head and traveled down my body. I reached up to touch the sensitive spot with my fingertips and was dismayed when they came back sticky with blood.

"Kevin, can you hand me a wet rag?" I asked, trying to keep my tone even so I wouldn't alarm him.

He nodded his head and grabbed the washcloth from the shower. He kept his eyes firmly on me as he anxiously wet the rag.

He handed it to me still dripping wet, but I didn't complain.

"Kevin, I think I have a concussion," I said after I washed the blood away as much as I could.

"What does that mean?" he asked frightened.

"It means my head is sick."

"Do you need to go to the hospital?"

"I don't think so, but I have a very important job for you."

"What is it?" He asked, standing up taller.

"I need you to make sure I don't fall asleep again. Do you think you can do that?"

"Why?"

"I'm not sure exactly, but I know from watching TV shows they always talk about how you shouldn't fall asleep."

"Is it bad that you already fell asleep?" Kevin asked worriedly.

"I don't think so, bud. Why don't we go to my room and we can read some more of 'Harry Potter and the Goblet of Fire.'"

"Does your head hurt too much to read?"

"I was going to let you read to me. You're reading skills put mine to shame anyway," I added, making him flush at my praise.

"Yeah, right."

"I'm serious. If I was half the reader you are when I was nine, I'd be a genius."

"You think so?" He asked as we settled in on my bed.

"Of course I do, champ, you're one smart guy."

"I don't feel all that smart sometimes in class."

"That's not your fault, bud. It's because we've moved so much and missed so much school. If we never moved you'd be running circles around the other kids with your grades."

"Katelyn, I wish it was someday soon now."

"Me too," I said, saddened at how defeated he sounded.

"Someday soon, it will be just us," he said, opening up his book where we had previously left off. "Well, Max too, if you want," he added, mentioning Max for the first time in weeks.

I could tell by the look he shot me he had been giving this a great deal of thought. I was amazed that even at nine he had a firm grasp of what was going on.

"I think that ship has sailed," I said, trying to make a joke of it.

"Nah, I saw the way he looked at you. He loves you."

"Very funny, we hardly knew each other. How would you know about that anyway?"

"Did you love him?"

I debated avoiding his question before I finally answered it honestly. "I think it was too early for love, but I liked him more than anyone else I've ever known."

"Even me?" Kevin asked seriously.

"No, bud, I could never like anyone more than you," I answered, reassuring him.

"More than Mom?" he persisted.

"Yeah, more than Mom. Come on, stop stalling and read," I said before the conversation went any deeper. It was one thing for me to feel nothing for Lucinda, but I didn't want to influence Kevin in that way. It was up to him how he wanted to feel.

Taking my hint, Kevin began to read. I was amazed at how much his fluency had increased since our move here and only had to help him occasionally with the harder words.

"Mom's like Harry's aunt and uncle," Kevin said as we took a break to munch on some sandwiches he had made for our dinner.

"Nah, at least she doesn't make us sleep in a broom closet."

"Yeah, but she does treat us badly," he said after swallowing a bite of his sandwich.

"That's true. Hmm, maybe our letters to Hogwarts will arrive any day now," I teased.

"That would rock," Kevin said before going into a whole tirade about how cool it would be to live in the castle and be able to eat good food all the time.

We read through the night and Kevin was my hero as he made sure to shake me awake each time my eyes drifted closed. Lucinda strolled in sometime after midnight, but neither Kevin nor I made a move to leave my room. By six a.m. I finally felt it was safe for me to fall asleep, so Kevin and I fell into an exhausted slumber and slept through the entire day. We both woke at dinnertime, and I made us both something easy since my head was still pounding like a drum. Once our bellies were full, we both headed back to bed and slept through the rest of the night.

Sunday morning Lucinda was awake when I stumbled out to the living room to get myself something to drink. I saw her take in my appearance, pausing at my head which had dried blood caked throughout the strands of hair where the wound had bled while I slept. She didn't acknowledge me other than her stare, and I followed suit. I was used to the silent treatment. If Lucinda lashed out at me because she was mad at someone else, she was usually remorseful the next day. If she lashed out at me because I had defied her, she would spend several days afterwards giving me the silent treatment until I apologized.

I headed to the bathroom to clean up with my drink in hand. My reflection in the mirror told the whole story. With dried blood throughout my hair and down my neck, I looked like I had stepped out of some horror movie. Reaching in to start the shower, I gasped when I saw rust colored water inside the tub.

"MOM!" I yelled, forgetting she was giving me the silent treatment. "MOM!"

"What?" she said, obviously aggravated I had interrupted her vow of silence.

"There's something wrong with the shower," I said, pointing at the inch high smelly water that sat in the tub.

Without saying anything, she twisted the knob at the sink, but nothing came out.

"Did we not pay the water bill?" I asked confused.

"No, the pipes are frozen."

"Get out, seriously?" I asked.

"Yeah, it happened when we lived in Colorado when you were a baby."

"What do we do? Do you need to call the landlord?"

"Um, no," she said, heading out of the bathroom.

"Why not?" I asked, sensing she was hiding something from me. "I'm sure he'd send someone out to fix it," I said, stating the obvious.

"Because, Miss Know-It-All, we still owe this month's rent," she said, stomping down the hall.

"Are we going to pay it?" I asked, thinking I was playing with fire again.

"Not unless you have some hidden stash of money I don't know about," she said in a snarky voice as she sat on the couch and lit up another cigarette.

"I thought we didn't have to pay rent here for a while?" I asked, grasping at straws.

"It was for two months," she said, taking a long draw on her cigarette. "God, Katelyn, stop being a worrywart, we've been in worse situations than this. They'll release Jim on Monday, and he'll find another job."

I sat down heavily on the coffee table, trying to digest her words. "What do we do about the pipes?" I finally asked as she stubbed out her cigarette.

"Nothing we can do. You need to run over and get a plunger from the grocery store, so we can take care of the mess in the tub. I'd stop at the gas station first to clean up if I were you," she said, not taking responsibility for the blood that caked my hair.

"Whatever," I mumbled, standing up.

I woke Kevin once I returned to my room so he could go with me to the gas station to use the bathroom.

"Why do we have to pee there?" Kevin asked as we pulled our heavy coats on.

"Because the pipes are frozen here," I said. "Frozen pipes mean no water, which means no water to flush a toilet," I added, pulling his hat down over his ears.

"Can't I just pee outside?" he asked logically.

"You could, but I figured we might as well brush our teeth and wash up so we both don't have to do it later," I said, holding up the bag of toiletries I had packed.

"Grrr, I thought we wouldn't have to use gas station bathrooms as long as we lived here," he grumbled, pulling on his gloves.

"I know pal, me too. Such is our life, though."

Kevin trailed behind me, still grumpy about leaving the somewhat warmth of the trailer. I opened the door and gasped as a frigid breeze blew through the door.

"Holy crapinoli, it's cold out here," Kevin grumbled as we walked against the breeze.

"Let's hurry," I said, agreeing with him. I grasped his hand, dragging him along as we fought the wind that seemed hell-bent on pushing us back.

"Katelyn, it's too cold," Kevin complained through chattering teeth as we approached the small intersection.

"We're almost there," I said loudly over the howling wind and swirling snow that was being blown recklessly around our faces.

Kevin slipped right after we stepped into the road. The momentum of his fall dragged me down and made me land smartly on my backside.

I struggled to catch my breath as Kevin started to giggle beside me.

"Not funny, punk," I said, trying to rise without slipping again. "We're in the middle of the road," I scolded him, trying to be the mature one.

"Hehehe, not like it matters,'" he said, still laughing. "We're the only stupid ones out here," he said, indicating the deserted roads.

He had a point. The wind had blown the snow into huge drifts in some areas while other areas were left completely barren and not a single soul was around. If not for the light shining behind the ice-covered window of the gas station with Old Man Wither behind the counter, I would have believed we were the only people left on Earth.

"Well, it doesn't mean we should hang out in the middle of the road like buffoons," I said, dragging him the rest of the way across the street.

Old Man Wither, as everyone liked to call him, greeted us with astonishment as we burst through the door, anxious to escape the treacherous conditions outside. "What in the blazes are you youngsters doing out there?" he asked, coming around the counter to see us.

"Our pipes froze," Kevin said, scurrying off to use the bathroom.

"Frozen pipes? That's a tough one. Did you folks forget to leave a tap running?" he asked, pouring a tall cup of hot chocolate and handing it to me.

"Oh no, I can't," I said, trying to decline the beverage.

"It's on the house, young lady. You young'uns shouldn't be out in this weather. I told Meryl not to even come in today."

"So, if you run water your pipes won't freeze?" I asked, returning to his earlier question.

"Most times it works," he said, leaning back against a waist-high soda cooler that sat in the middle of the floor. "Hey, that's a pretty nasty cut you have on your head there," he added, studying me intently.

"Um, yeah, I tripped and hit it on the coffee table," I lied, mentally kicking myself for neglecting to pull my hood up over my head.

"I'm sure. I had plenty of those injuries myself when I was growing up," he said, looking at me knowingly.

"She thinks she had a concassion," Kevin said, closing the bathroom door behind him.

"Concussion," I corrected him, wishing he'd kept that information to himself.

"Did you blackout?" Old Man Wither asked.

I nodded my head. "For a few minutes."

"Sick to your stomach?" He asked, stepping closer to inspect my wound.

I nodded my head again.

"Yep, sounds like you gave yourself a fine one," he said, gently probing at my head. "Young man," he said, looking at Kcvin. "I keep a first aid kit behind the counter. Can you grab it for me?"

"Sure," Kevin asked, delighted to help out.

"Really, I'm fine," I started to protest.

"I'm sure you are, missy, but an injury like this needs to be taken care of, unless you rather I run you up to the hospital," he said, making his point clear.

"No, that's okay," I replied, stepping closer so he could see my injury better.

"Kevin, grab me a bottle of water too from that stack over there," he said, pointing to a display of water sitting off to the side of the counter.

I watched as he opened the first aid kit and removed a large gauze pad. Using his teeth, he tore the corner off the package and extracted the sterile pad. He used the water to douse the pad before gently applying it to my head.

My eyes watered as the pad touched the injury.

"I know it stings, but we need to see what we're dealing with," he said, cleaning the area as gently as possible. "Looks like you could use some stitches," he said, studying my head critically. "You sure you don't want me to run you up to the county hospital?"

"I'm sure," I said earnestly, looking at Kevin possessively.

He followed my gaze. "I see," he said. "Well, let's see what I can do."

I sighed in relief as he let the subject go and let him lead me to his stool so I could perch there while he worked on my head.

"I'm going to have to shave a little of your hair away from the cut so we can get the bleeding to stop," he said, waiting to get my permission.

I nodded, cringing slightly at the thought of having a bald spot.

"Don't go worrying your pretty head. All your other hair will cover it up just fine."

He worked without talking after that, deftly trimming the hair that surrounded my cut and then set to work on closing it up. I almost lost my nerve when I saw him pull out a bottle of super glue.

"Trust me dear, if you were at the hospital they'd use the same thing," he said, patting my shoulder.

"Oh sweet Katelyn, he's gluing your head," Kevin said, laughing like it was the most hysterical thing he had ever heard.

"Can you use it on his mouth?" I asked Old Man Wither sweetly.

"Sure can," he winked, advancing on Kevin who slapped his hands over his mouth as his body shook with suppressed laughter.

Mr. Wither chuckled, turning back to me. "Okay, looks good. I guess it's a blessing your water is out since you need to keep the injury relatively dry. Why don't you go take a look at it?"

"Okay," I said, heading for the bathroom.

Entering the small, surprisingly clean gas station bathroom, I flipped the light switch, making the fluorescent bulbs hum above my head. I relieved my bladder before turning to the mirror to study Old Man Wither's handiwork. Parting my hair, I studied the wound critically and could see why he had suggested stitches. The cut was easily over an inch long. The glue gave it a grotesque appearance, but I was grateful he was able to close it up without making a fuss about it needing stitches.

Once I was satisfied my wound couldn't be seen, I dipped my fingers in the warm tap water and combed them through my hair trying to remove the last traces of dried blood. It was tedious work, but finally after several minutes, I was satisfied that the majority of it was gone. I stripped my jacket and hoodie off and stood shivering in the bathroom as I used the washcloth I had brought along to wash my face, arms and neck. Feeling slightly cleaner, I pulled my jacket back on to ward off the chills and brushed my teeth vigorously before returning all my items back to the toiletry bag.

"Hey, Kevin, come brush your teeth," I said, opening the bathroom door only to discover Kevin in the middle of munching on a hotdog.

"Look at what Mr. Wither gave me," he said between bites.

"That's great, bud, now hurry and eat it so you can brush your teeth."

"Done," he said, finishing off the last bite in one gulp. He snagged the bag from my hand before trotting happily off to the bathroom, leaving Mr. Wither and me alone.

"Um, thanks for giving him a hotdog. I'll pay you as soon as we have the money," I said, flushing in embarrassment.

He held up his hand to stop my tirade. "It's my treat," he said as I tried to protest. "Now you listen here, since my dear Marge decided it was time to meet our maker, I haven't had a single moment as entertaining as the one I spent with you young'ns this morning. My Marge and I were never blessed with kids, but I would like to hope if we had been, they would have been like you two."

"What makes you say that?" I asked curiously.

"Let's just say I can tell about people, and my door here is always open if you and your brother there need anything. Got me? Lord knows I can always use the company if you ever want to chat."

"Thanks," I mumbled.

He patted my shoulder. "Trust me when I say this is just a small part of your life, so you keep your chin up," he said, offering words of wisdom.

"I know," I said, swallowing the lump in my throat. "We better head out," I added as Kevin joined me.

"Ready to brave the elements again, bud?" I said as I zipped up Kevin's jacket.

"Not really," Kevin answered, grimacing as the wind continued to swirl outside.

The trek to the store was tougher than the one to the gas station since we had to cross the icy roads twice to get to the far corner. We both sighed with pleasure when we stumbled inside the store, allowing the warmth to defrost our frozen bodies. My sighs of relief were cut short when I spotted Max chatting with his father near the registers.

Ours eyes met as he hungrily took in my appearance. I slid my hoodie up over my head self-consciously, worried that my hair wasn't properly covering my injury. After a moment, I finally pulled my eyes away, dragging Kevin along on our hunt for a plunger. After finding what we needed, I took a deep breath, preparing myself for what would be a long awkward walk up to the nearly-deserted front area of the store. As my rotten luck would have it, Kevin and I were the only customers here. Obviously, no one else in town was foolish enough to venture outside with conditions so dismal.

Max's dad scanned the plunger through while Max bagged it for us.

"Plumbing problems?" his dad asked conversationally.

"Pipes are frozen," Kevin piped in.

"That sucks," Max said as I handed a five over to his dad.

"Yeah, it does. We..." Kevin started to say as I clamped a hand down on his shoulder before he could embarrass me further.

"Dad, you think Harold could go take a look at it?" Max asked as he handed me my bag.

"Not until the weather warms up a bit."

"That's okay, I'm sure the owner has someone he can send out," I said, edging toward the door.

"You two didn't walk over here, did you?" his dad asked, his brows coming together in concern.

"Yep, we did, and it's freeeeeezing out there," Kevin said, exaggerating the word before I could stop him.

"Max, go pull up the truck. There's no way I'm letting you two walk back home," he said sternly as I started to protest.

"No arguments, please. The only reason we ventured out today is so I could send the staff home and lock up the building. We're under a severe storm advisory. Looks like schools will be closed the last few days before winter break was supposed to begin anyway."

"Woohoo, really?" Kevin asked, pumping his fist in the air enthusiastically.

Max's dad chuckled. "Spoken like a true kid," he said, shooting me a smile. "Looks like Max is ready," he added, indicating the vehicle idling outside the front doors. "You two have a nice holiday," he said kindly.

"You too," I said, before herding Kevin out the door.

Max had the heat cranked up all the way when Kevin and I climbed up into the vehicle.

"Yes, it's so nice and warm in here," Kevin said, slumping back in the seat. "I'm never getting out," he added, closing his eyes.

"What if we run out of gas," Max said, laughing easily.

"I'd just make you park it over at Old Man Wither's," Kevin countered.

"Yeah, but you'd be sad when you got hungry, wouldn't you?"

"Nah, Old Man Wither has the best hotdogs ever."

Max roared with laughter over Kevin's logic. "I guess you've got a point, bud," he said, obviously enjoying the easy comradeship they shared.

Listening to them banter back and forth didn't help my broken heart. It was pure bliss and agony at the same time to be so close to him after I had carefully kept myself distanced from him over the last few months.

Max pulled up in front of our trailer and Kevin jumped out, obviously forgetting his resolve to stay in the vehicle forever.

I reached for my own door handle. "Thanks for the ride," I said as I started to climb out of the vehicle. Max reached over and grasped my arm. "Don't," I whispered, looking down at his hand that seemed to burn through my multiple layers of clothing.

"Why? Does my touch disgust you?" he asked in the husky voice that sent my heart into overdrive.

I shook my head no.

"Then why?" he asked earnestly as I pulled my arm from his grasp.

"Because it makes me forget everything else," I said quietly, climbing from the vehicle. I looked back for an instant, watching him study me intently before closing the trailer door.

Chapter 11

School was closed the following day as the storm outside continued to rage. The gusting winds caused the trailer to shimmy and shake like an amusement park ride. Kevin and I stayed bundled up together in my room reading, only venturing out once to use the bathroom at Mr. Wither's place. He greeted us enthusiastically, making us each a cup of hot chocolate before we trekked back home. Lucinda spent the majority of the day on the phone swearing as she tried in vain to get Jim released. It appeared that Jim's boss didn't take kindly to being stolen from and had decided to press charges. Lucinda was distraught when she found out that he was being moved to the county jail where he would most likely get six months to a year for his crime. I kept Kevin away from her as she raged through the house, breaking things in her frustration until she finally dissolved into a pile of tears.

Kevin watched me wide-eyed as I made us sandwiches for dinner. I worked to keep his mind off her loud crying by declaring we would be having an indoor picnic on my bed.

He picked at his food solemnly before finally pushing the barely eaten sandwich away.

"Not hungry, bud?" I asked, picking at my own sandwich.

"No, my tummy hurts," he said, lying back against my pillows.

"Oh, I'm sorry, bud. Everything's going to be fine," I said, trying to comfort him.

He nodded his head, but I could tell the weight of Lucinda's outburst throughout the day had worn on him.

He closed his eyes and drifted off to sleep with one hand resting against his flat stomach. I brushed my hand across his forehead to make sure he didn't have a fever and was relieved that it felt cool to the touch.

I carried our leftover dinner to the kitchen and dumped the plates into the trash. Once I returned to my room, I shut off my light and carefully climbed into the bed beside Kevin so I wouldn't disturb him. I felt like I had just shut my eyes when Kevin shook me awake.

"Katelyn, I have to go to the bathroom."

"Okay, I'll let you pee outside," I said groggily rubbing the sleep from my eyes.

"No, I have to go to the bathroom," he said plaintively as I switched on the light.

"Oh no," I said, taking in his pinched pale face. "Okay, let me get your jacket," I said, rushing into his room.

I hastily stuffed Kevin into his jacket, watching his face continue to pale even further. After dragging his stocking hat onto his head, I shrugged into my own jacket and helped him down the hall.

I gasped when I opened the front door and the wind whipped viciously around us. Kevin seemed oblivious to it, walking hunched over from what must have been severe stomach cramps. We were halfway across the street when he started vomiting. I rubbed his back trying to comfort him as he expelled all the contents from his belly.

"Do you still need the bathroom?" I asked anxiously, keeping an eye out for any approaching vehicles.

He nodded his head miserably.

"Okay, we're almost there," I said, herding him the rest of the way across the street.

It was only after we were standing directly in front of the gas station did the lack of lighting inside the building finally sink in. I groaned in dismay. I hadn't even bothered to check the time before we had headed out.

"Katelyn," Kevin moaned, looking at the dark building.

I felt hopeless as we stood in front of the empty building, shivering uncontrollably in our pajamas. After a moment of indecisiveness, I grabbed Kevin's gloved hand and dragged him around the side of the building to the back where Old Man Wither's small house was located. Not knowing what else to do, I knocked loudly on the front door. I felt incredibly guilty for waking him, but the pained look on Kevin's face prompted me to knock again even louder.

The door pulled open abruptly before I could knock a third time and a blurry-eyed Mr. Wither stared bewildered at us.

"I'm sooooooo sorry to disturb you sir, but my brother is sick and your gas station is closed. Can he please use yours?" The words tumbled out of my lips in a rush. "I'm sorry," I repeated as he stared at us for a moment blankly until Kevin moaned again.

"Yes, yes, come in," he said, moving aside so we could step into his warm house.

He ushered Kevin to the bathroom, leaving me to stand awkwardly in the entryway. After a moment, he joined me.

"Come on in and have a seat," he said, settling into a large mocha-colored leather recliner.

"Thank you so much, Mr. Wither," I said, sitting on the edge of the sofa that matched the recliner. "I didn't know what else to do," I added.

"That's fine, dear. Anytime you need it, you let me know. My Marge would have had my head for not offering it sooner. That goes for the shower too."

I looked down at the floor uncomfortably, suddenly leery about seeking out the help of a man, no matter how kind he seemed.

"Katelyn, I mean while I'm working in the store," he added, sensing my unease.

"Sorry," I said as relief flowed through me. I hated that I was always initially skeptical of other people and often wondered if I would have turned out differently if I would have had a normal childhood. "That's kind of you to offer," I added.

"Anytime, my dear. Like I said, my Marge would have had my head for not offering sooner. I'll leave the door unlocked for you two. You don't even have to stop through the station if it makes you uncomfortable."

"Thanks," I said again, overwhelmed at his generosity.

"Your mama, though, ain't welcome as far as I'm concerned, crackin' your head and all," he said seriously.

I nodded my head, not bothering to deny it. I had known when he took care of me that he had seen through my lie.

"You could report her. Nowadays the law doesn't take kindly to child beaters."

"They would separate Kevin and me," I replied, making my point clear.

"I reckon you're right. They always seem to have the best of intentions, but don't know how to pull their heads out of their butts long enough to do it right."

His words cracked me up. "That's true," I said, glad he understood.

"So, what's your plan?"

"I just need to turn eighteen, and then I'll fight her for him," I said, confiding in him.

"That could be tough without money and such."

"I'm a hard worker, and I know how to survive," I said defensively.

"Oh, I'm sure you are, dear. I'm just saying it's going to be tough, trust me," he said earnestly.

"Did you do it?" I asked.

"Yup, I raised my two younger brothers. My dad's belt seemed to be a permanent fixture to his hand. I suffered many beatings being the oldest. I pulled up stakes when he started using the belt freely on my youngest brother."

"And you guys made it okay?" I asked, intrigued about his story.

"It was tough at first, but then I met Marge and she helped me raise up my brothers until they went off to college."

"Wow, where are they now?"

"One's a doctor over in Bozeman, and the other is a wildlife specialist in Yellowstone," he said proudly.

"Wow," I repeated, impressed that his brothers had turned out so well. My worst fear was that Kevin would fall through the cracks and never find his true potential.

"I'll tell you what, when your moment comes, you look me up. My Marge and I set money aside for such a situation."

"Oh no, I could never take your money," I protested.

"It's not my money, sweetheart, it's yours. That's what Marge would have wanted. It broke her heart when she found out she couldn't bear her own children, so she threw herself into showering all her love onto those less unfortunate. You ask my brothers Hank and Tommy and they'd claim she was a saint," he said with bright eyes as he looked at the picture on the table beside his chair.

"Can I see?" I asked

"Sure, this is my Marge on our wedding day," he said, handing over a picture of a couple standing at the alter with two teenage boys next to them. The woman in the picture had rich auburn hair that seemed to float around her. The dress she wore was simple, but her poise made it very elegant.

"She was beautiful," I said sincerely.

"That she was. What she saw in a ragamuffin like me, I'll never know."

"I'm sure she saw something," I said, studying the picture of him that was easily more than thirty years old. Strangely enough, he wore the same look on his face that I often had on mine, and I came to realize it was the look of someone who had the weight of the world on their shoulders. He and I were two peas in a pod.

"Katelyn, can we go home?" Kevin asked, joining us.

"Sure bud, are you feeling better?"

"A little, I threw up again too."

"I'm sorry bud," I said, standing up.

Old Man Wither held up a hand. "Now you just sit here for a moment. I'm going to go warm up my pickup truck and I'll drive you two home."

"You don't have to do that," I tried to protest.

"I wouldn't have it any other way. Your mother should be tarred and feathered for letting you two come out on a night like this."

Kevin joined me on the couch and laid his head in my lap as Mr. Wither headed out the front door to warm up his truck.

I brushed Kevin's hair back off his forehead, grimacing at how pale and clammy his complexion was.

"What's tar and feather mean?" he asked weakly, keeping his eyes shut.

"It's just a phrase from a long time ago," I said, skirting around its real origin.

Mr. Wither joined us, shaking snow from his head.

"Is it snowing?" I asked.

"Nah, the wind is just blowin' the snowdrifts around something fierce," he said, reaching out a hand to help Kevin up.

Old Man Wither dropped us off at our trailer steps after making me promise to call him the next time we needed the bathroom in the middle of the night, so he could pick us up. I agreed, though I knew I would never take him up on it. He had already gone above and beyond for us.

Chapter 12

Lucinda fell into a complete funk the days leading up to Christmas. She locked herself in her room, only emerging every once in a great while to shuffle across the street to use the bathroom. I left food outside her door and several hours later the used utensils would appear outside her door again. This was new territory for us since we were used to her dumping someone when she was ready to move on. We were stuck in limbo since Lucinda was obviously not ready to trade Jim in for a newer model, but she also wasn't capable of functioning on her own. She left the house only once to visit Jim and didn't return until late that night, and as Christmas approached, her mood only worsened as she cut off Kevin and me completely.

Kevin and I took advantage of her reclusiveness, spending hours reading, playing games and watching the TV that I had moved back to the living room. Kevin recovered quickly from his stomach bug and soon began to out-eat me as he was finally able to enjoy his meals without the normal stresses. Our food supply had shrunk to nothing by the time the storm began to dissipate outside.

The day before Christmas Eve, I knew it was time to hit up Lucinda for her food stamp card so I could replenish our pantry and get something special to make for Christmas day.

I knocked on her door tentatively, not sure what to expect.

"What?" she demanded through the door.

"I need to ask you something," I said, sliding the door open.

"What?" she said, not bothering to look up from her computer where she was furiously typing.

"I need your food stamp card," I said, aggravated with her tone.

"There's no money on it," she said, still not looking at me.

"What?" I asked incredulously. "They put more money on it on the tenth," I said, knowing for a fact there should still be well over three hundred dollars on it.

"I traded in the balance for cash so I could buy cigarettes for Jim and me," she said, taking a long draw on her cigarette to emphasize the point.

"What do you mean you traded for cash?"

"I mean, I found some guy Jim recommended in Bozeman that would give me cash for the credit on my card, Miss I-Need-To-Know-Everything."

"And there's nothing left?" I asked, letting her derogatory comment slide. I did the quick math in my head and my mouth dried up when I realized we wouldn't get it replenished again for seventeen days. "What about the cash? Did he give you the whole three hundred?" I asked as hope flared up inside me.

She laughed at my question like I was a foolish child. "He pays twenty-five cents on the dollar."

"You traded three hundred dollars we had for food for seventy-five bucks, so you could buy cigarettes?" I asked, feeling the urge to puke.

She nodded and resumed typing on the computer as if I wasn't there.

I left the room before I said anything that would turn into a battle and upset Kevin.

I hate her. I hate her. I hate her! The words ran through my head as I sunk onto my bed, searching for a solution. I couldn't take the car and drive to a food bank since Lucinda had never bothered to take me in to get my license. I could ask Old Man Wither to take me, but I hated to impose on him more than we already had. I left my room so I could survey the cupboards more thoroughly to see if I had missed anything.

My disappointment and panic rose as I saw that the contents of the cabinets were as dire as I originally thought. Only the one box of mac and cheese that I planned on us eating for lunch remained. I had used the last of the bread and peanut butter for our breakfast that morning and mentally kicked myself for fixing Lucinda any.

"Katelyn, are we going to the store?" Kevin asked, bundled up in his outside garb.

"Um, not right now bud," I said, sinking down on the kitchen chair.

"What's the matter?" he asked.

"Nothing," I said, trying to smile.

"She spent the money," he said, wise beyond his years. "What can we do?"

"I'm going to see if Lucinda will drive me to the food bank," I said, trying to reassure him.

"Mom said the car has no gas."

"That's right. Damn it. I frikin' forgot that!" I said as my frustration at Lucinda escalated.

"It's okay, Katelyn, how many times before did we not have any food? Lots." Kevin said, patting my arm.

His comfort was my undoing, and I laid my head back, wishing I could cry. Kevin continued to pat my back like an adult would. I felt wretched letting him see me so down, but I was so sick of nothing ever working out.

"Come on, let's go," he said, pulling me up from the chair.

"To where?" I asked, completely confused.

"We're going to Old Man Wither's. He said if we ever needed anything to come see him," Kevin said logically.

"Okay," I said, not daring to question his logic. I could tell he was trying to be the stronger one.

Mr. Wither wasn't in the gas station so Kevin and I tromped through the snowdrifts to get to his front door.

"Bathroom?" Mr. Wither said as a greeting when he opened the door.

"No, we need your help," Kevin said, puffing out his chest and standing tall.

Mr. Wither smiled at him and glanced at me. His smile disappeared as he took in my gloomy expression. "Are you hurt?" he asked, herding us into his house.

"No, but we want to know if you can give us a ride to the food bank," Kevin said, still speaking for me. "We'll help work around the store to help pay for the gas. Right, Katelyn?" he said, looking at me.

"Absolutely," I agreed, smiling slightly at his bravado.

"Well, I'm sure I can think of a few odd jobs you could do around here," Old Man Wither said with a twinkle in his eye. "But I reckon a round trip to Bozeman in my old beat-up truck would run us close to fifty dollars in gas. I'm thinking it'd be much easier if I give you cash and you and your sister can get a few things you need from the store here," he said to Kevin, not leaving room for me to protest.

"I reckon that makes sense," Kevin said, picking up Wither's phrase.

I couldn't help but giggle as Old Man Wither roared with laughter. "Sounds like a done deal to me," he finally said when he stopped laughing.

He reached into his back pocket and pulled out his wallet. He counted out five twenties and handed them to Kevin, not looking at me. I wanted to protest, but knew that it would fall on deaf ears. Besides, could I really deny Kevin the nourishment his underweight body so dearly needed?

"I'll pay it back," I promised.

"I know you will, my dear," he said, patting my shoulder.

"Come on, I'll give you a lift over to the store. I need to have a meeting with Maxwell anyway."

"Woohoo," Kevin said, jumping up and down with excitement like the walk across the street was just too far for him.

Old Man Wither left Kevin and me at the front door so we could start our shopping while he headed toward the management offices at the far front corner of the store.

Kevin and I made quick work of our shopping, buying only the essentials to get us through the next few weeks. We got our usual staple items like generic peanut butter, Top Ramen soup, mac and cheese, and several frozen dollar pizzas. I resented that I had to add girlie products to the cart, but there was no arguing with stinking Mother Nature. The only impulse item I allowed us to get was a rotisserie chicken for Christmas Day. I planned on serving it with peas, rolls and mashed potatoes, but chafed at the idea of spending ten dollars for one meal, especially since Kevin and I would be out of school for two weeks and would be eating breakfast and lunch at home. Kevin was a sport during the shopping trip and found it a game to find the cheapest priced items he could.

"How about these for dinner one night?" he asked, holding up a can of Vienna sausages.

"Gag, no thanks," I said, making a gagging noise to emphasis my point.

He giggled at my response. "Okay, how about these?" he asked, holding up a can of sardines.

"Are you nuts?" I said as we both burst out laughing at the same time.

"Well, you said we needed to eat cheap. You get like six little fishes in this one can," he added, smiling at me impishly.

"I'd rather eat dirt," I said, ruffling his hair as we headed for the next aisle.

"Yum, can we have spaghetti?" he pleaded, holding up a big jar of his favorite sauce.

"Sure, but without any meat," I said, feeling bad when his face drooped momentarily in disappointment.

"Okay," he said, rebounding quickly.

I grabbed several boxes of different pasta noodles off the shelf since they were buy one, get one free and added the biggest jar of sauce they had, figuring it would get us through several meals.

"Well, that should do us," I said, pushing the full buggy to the front of the store.

"Can I get a candy bar?" Kevin asked, eyeing the multiple rows of chocolate near the register.

"We'll see," I said out of the corner of my mouth as Max stepped up to the end of the conveyor belt to bag our stuff. I was mortified as he diplomatically bagged up my personal hygiene items.

"How's it going, Kevin?"

"Hey, Max," Kevin said happily, abandoning his stakeout by the candy to give Max an uncharacteristic hug around the waist.

I watched Kevin come alive as he and Max bagged up the groceries together, easily falling into their favorite conversation about superheroes. I tried not to be obvious as my eyes drank in Max's appearance. It had only been a few days since I had seen him, but my heart kicked into overdrive as he threw his head back to laugh at something Kevin said.

"Cash or charge, sweetie?" Susan, the nicest of the cashiers asked, interrupting my gawking session.

"Cash," I said, pulling my eyes reluctantly from Max. "Oh, Kevin, you can pick a candy bar," I said, noticing we had just over four dollars left over.

"Sweet," Kevin said, grabbing his favorite brand.

"Do you need a lift home?" Max asked.

"No, Old Man Wither said he'd take us home," I said, pointing toward Mr. Wither as he exited Max's dad's office.

"Oh, okay," Max said, sounding disappointed. "Have a good Christmas then," he said, ruffling Kevin's hair.

"Thanks, you too," Kevin said as I choked back a sudden lump in my throat. I yearned for things to be different. I missed his touch more acutely than I had ever missed anything in all the years that I had left cherished items behind.

"Katelyn," Max said, reaching out to grab my hand. His touch was as warm and soft as I remembered it.

"Yeah?" I asked, making the mistake of looking up into his eyes.

"Have a great Christmas," he said as the pad of his thumb gently rubbed the top of my hand.

"You too Max," I said with sudden weak knees as he continued to hold my hand.

"Let's go, Katelyn," Kevin said, standing by the atrium doors that kept the cold temperatures from flowing in every time someone opened the door.

"I have to go," I said, stating the obvious.

"Right," Max said, finally releasing my hand.

My hand felt irrationally lost without his. *Like I was missing a limb*, I couldn't help thinking as I slowly walked toward Kevin.

Old Man Wither helped us carry the groceries through the frigid temperatures into our trailer that felt only slightly warmer.

"Might bit chilly in here. Don't you think?" he asked, rubbing his hands together.

"A little," I said, trying to sound blasé. "The heat's been acting up since the storm started. I'm sure the landlord will send someone out to fix it," I said, not wanting to admit that Lucinda had neglected to pay the rent.

"Hmmm, who knows when he'll be able to get a repairman out here with it being the holidays and such," Mr. Wither said. "I'm going to run over to the station and grab some tools so I can take a look at it."

"No really, you don't have to do that. We wouldn't want to trouble you more than we already have," I said, shooting an uneasy glance down the hall at Lucinda's closed door.

"It's no trouble, and I won't be in your hair since the unit's outside," he said, looking at me meaningfully.

"Are you sure?" I asked quietly.

"Positive, my dear," he said, heading out the door.

I was halfway through making dinner when the air that had been pumping through the floorboard vents began to warm up instantly, taking the chill of the interior of the trailer.

"Yay, Katelyn, we have heat," Kevin said, sitting on the vent in the living room.

"Well, don't block it, dork," I said, laughing at him.

I expected to hear Old Man Wither's pickup rumble to life as it pulled out, but the sound never came. It wasn't until I was washing our silverware with a jug of water that I kept by the sink that I heard a soft knock on the trailer door.

Drying my hands on the back of my jeans, I walked to the front door and pulled it open.

"Mr. Wither, I thought you left an hour ago," I said, surprised to see him.

"Nah, there were a few other things I wanted to take care of. Why don't you go turn on the kitchen faucet and see if anything comes out."

Excitedly, I rushed to the kitchen sink, not daring to believe. When I twisted the knob, I giggled in delight as water poured from the faucet. My giggles turned to happy tears as I realized that Kevin and I would no longer have to trek across the street at all hours of the night to go potty.

Mr. Wither joined me in the kitchen. "Very good," he said, twisting the knob to high to check the water pressure. "Now, just keep this one running at a trickle when the temperatures dip too low and that should keep the pipes from freezing again," he added.

"Thank you so much," I said, throwing my arms around him.

"No problem, my dear," he said, patting my back uncomfortably. "Don't go being strangers now that it's fixed, though," he told Kevin and me sternly as he headed for the front door.

"We won't," I reassured him, walking him to his truck. "Thank you so much for all your help today. You've single-handedly saved Christmas for us now that my stepdad is away..." I added, letting my voice trail off for the last part.

"Did he go away on business?"

"Not really," I said, skirting away from the truth.

"Will he be home by tomorrow?"

"Um no, I don't think so," I said, avoiding his eyes.

"Well, you two take care, and have yourself a nice night."

"You too, Mr. Wither, and thanks again for everything," I said, shutting the door behind me quickly so none of our new blissful heat could escape.

"Alright, bud, I'm going to go scour out the tub, and then you can take a nice hot shower," I said, grinning at Kevin happily.

"Woohoo, no more freezing our butts off to go potty," Kevin crowed, following me to the bathroom. He perched on the closed toilet seat chattering away as I cleaned out the tub.

I smiled at his glee. It didn't take much to make us happy. All we needed were the basic human necessities: food, shelter, water and heat, and we were good to go.

It took a lot of elbow grease to finally remove the rancid ring that had formed along the inside of the tub. I used the Comet liberally, making sure the tub sparkled before I would allow Kevin to use it.

Chapter 13

Kevin and I both went to bed cleaner than we had been in days and when I woke the next morning, I saw that Lucinda had also enjoyed our windfall by the towels she had left scattered around the bathroom. Her depression over Jim's incarceration hadn't lifted, but I was relieved she was at least making an attempt to keep herself clean. I gathered her used towels and as many of our dirty clothes that would fit into one load of laundry.

I made Kevin go with me to the laundry room at the far end of the trailer park so he could get some fresh air. He followed behind carrying the jug of laundry soap and purposefully slid across the light dusting of snow that had fallen the night before while we were sleeping.

"Do you think Lucinda will let us open our presents tonight?" Kevin asked after a few minutes.

"I don't know," I said, shifting the weight of the duffle bag filled with our dirty clothes to my other shoulder. "I'm not sure she'll be joining us for Christmas. I'll tell you what though, if she doesn't come out of her room by nine o'clock tonight, I'll let you open one."

"Really?" he asked, skidding to a stop in front of me.

"Yeah really, but let's hurry to the laundromat so I can stop freezing my butt-kiss off."

He giggled at my choice of word.

"Besides, I want to get this laundry done so we can make Old Man Wither those brownies we bought last night."

"Yum, brownies. Can we have one toooooooo?" he pleaded.

"I think that can be arranged if you're a good helper."

"I will be. I promise," Kevin said, proving his point by holding the door of the small laundromat open for me.

Several hours later, Kevin held up to his promise as he helped me finish the laundry and prepare the brownies. By four in the afternoon, the trailer was spick-and-span and smelled heavenly from the double batch of brownies we had made up. I had felt massive guilt the day before, buying something as extravagant as brownies, but Kevin's enthusiasm made it totally worth it.

We bundled up in our winter clothes and trudged back through the snow with the plate of brownies we had set aside for Old Man Wither.

The gas station was closed up for the rest of the evening and the following day so we headed around the building to Mr. Wither's cabin. Kevin knocked on the door and said

"Merry Christmas" when a surprised Wither saw us standing on his doorstep.

"We made you brownies," I said, handing over the plate. "I know it's not much, but we just wanted to say thank you."

"Are you kidding me? This is the best gift I've gotten in years," he said, taking an appreciative whiff through the plastic wrap that covered them. "Come in, come in. I got a few things for you guys too. I was going to bring them over later, but now you've saved me the trip."

"Presents?" Kevin asked reverently.

"Yeah, presents," Mr. Wither said, leading us in through the front door. "Those ones are yours," he said to Kevin, pointing to a small stack at the far end of the coffee table.

Kevin squealed with glee when he saw his stack. "Can I open them?" he asked me pleadingly.

"Of course," I said, feeling an odd tickle in the back of my throat.

Needing no further encouragement, Kevin tore through his packages with shrieks of pure joy when he discovered a Nintendo DSI and several games to go with it.

"Um, Mr. Wither, that is way too generous of you," I said, mentally adding up the cost of Kevin's presents in my head.

"Oh shush, I haven't had this much fun shopping for presents in years. Me and my Marge would head to the shelter in Bozeman every Christmas and hand out gifts there. I haven't been much in the mood to keep up the tradition since her passing until now. So don't deprive an old man, okay?" he said with a twinkle in his eyes, making it obvious he was well aware of his nickname.

"Katelyn, look, it's a Marvel Hero game," Kevin said, stroking the package lovingly. Mr. Wither and I burst out laughing at the fawning look on his face.

"I guess you can tell he's pleased," I said, still giggling.

"Why don't you open yours," Mr. Wither said, handing me a present and a card. "Open the present first, though," he added, smiling at me.

"Okay," I said, suddenly uncomfortable. I couldn't recall the last time I had gotten a present, much less from someone who barcly knew mc.

Sensing my unease, Old Man Wither sank into his oversized recliner on the other side of the room, giving me the space I sought. I opened the present gently, taking care not to tear the paper since I planned on keeping it with a few items I had managed to slide past Lucinda over the years. The paper slowly gave away, revealing a rectangular-shaped box. My heart raced as I read the word "Kindle" across the carton. I had seen electronic book readers advertised on the TV but knew there was no way I would ever be able to get one.

"No way," I whispered, holding the item with trembling hands.

"You don't like it?" Old Man Wither asked worriedly. "Kevin told me you like to read."

"I love it, but there's no way I can accept it. It's way too expensive."

"Nah, the salesclerk said they've come way down in price since they were first released."

"It's the best thing I've ever gotten," I said truthfully, thinking about all the books I had abandoned over the years and the possibility of never having to do that again. My eyes filled with unshed tears of happiness at the thought. Embarrassed at my sudden wet eyes, I pulled up the flap of the envelope and extracted a funny Christmas card with a dancing reindeer on the cover. Opening it up, I discovered a fifty-dollar gift card to Amazon taped to the inside.

Before I could protest that it was too much, he held up his hand. "Now, the salesclerk also said there's a slew of books you can get for free, but I also wanted you to have a little money to get the books you want. No arguments, okay? You wouldn't want to deprive me of my first happy holiday in a long time, would you?"

"No," I said, still uncomfortable with the expense.

"Trust me, my dear, I bet my Marge is smiling down on us with approval," he said with sudden wet eyes.

"Well then, in that case, thank you so much. You'll never know how much this means to me," I said, hugging the carton close to my chest.

"How about a brownie?" Kevin asked in his typical exuberance.

"Sounds good to me," Mr. Wither said with a laugh, pulling the plastic wrap off the ceramic plate.

Kevin and I spent several hours with Old Man Wither as Kevin taught him the finer art of playing a handheld game system. While they took turns playing Marvel Heroes, I sat by the wall while my Kindle charged surfing through the automated manual. By the time Mr. Wither volunteered to take us home, I had found a mess of books I wanted to read. I was thrilled to see that tons of them were priced as low as ninety-nine cents.

Lucinda was still in her room when we returned home at nine, so I allowed Kevin to pick a present he wanted to open after we had sorted through them all. I wasn't surprised that Lucinda and Jim's own piles were twice as large as Kevin's and mine, but I was pleased that Kevin had almost a dozen for him alone.

"Your pile is pretty small," he said, looking at me worriedly.

"Hey, don't worry about it, pal. I got the best gift ever tonight thanks to you. If you wouldn't have told Old Man Wither I like to read, I would've never gotten this," I said, holding up my treasured Kindle. "So, which one are you going to open?"

"I think this one," he said, holding up a heavy, large rectangular box that had puzzled us for weeks.

"Okay," I said, secretly pleased the mystery of the package would be solved.

Kevin tore through the wrapping and opened the large carton beneath the paper. I swore under my breath when I saw him extract a baseball bat. Damn her! Lucinda was so intent on keeping Kevin from his love of action figures and superheroes that she would stoop so low to buy him something he had absolutely no use for.

Kevin shocked me by bursting out in laughter. "Wow, she really wants me to play sports," he said, looking at me with more understanding than someone his age should have.

"I guess so," I said honestly, looking at him with concern.

"Do you find it funny Mr. Withers knows us better than our own mom?" Kevin asked seriously as we turned off the living room light and headed for our rooms.

"Yeah, I do," I said, giving him a quick hug. "Merry Christmas Eve, bud."

"Merry Christmas Eve, Katelyn. I love you."

"I love you too, bud," I said as he slowly closed his bedroom door.

***

Kevin woke me early the next morning, excited to be celebrating the first Christmas morning with gifts that he could remember. I pretended to grumble about wanting to sleep in, but willingly allowed him to drag me out of bed. Lucinda didn't respond when we knocked on her bedroom door, so we headed to the living room without her.

"You open one first," Kevin said, handing me one of my six presents.

"How about we do them at the same time?" I suggested, knowing he was anxious to open his.

"Okay, ready, set, go," he said, tearing through the wrapping paper, making it fly everywhere.

I watched him for a minute, enjoying the moment. I'm sure most teenagers would have resented all the time they had to spend with their younger siblings, but I had been taking care of Kevin since he was born when I was eight. He was such an easy baby, hardly ever crying or demanding attention, so it was easy to bond with him. I could never remember a moment in my life when I had resented him. Even when I suffered Lucinda's wrath, the payoff seemed worth it if Kevin was protected.

"Katelyn, open yours," Kevin demanded, breaking me reverie.

Focusing on him, I saw that he had already opened his presents. "Oops, sorry bud, I guess I'm still sleepy. What did you get?"

Kevin showed me all his gifts that ran along the same theme as the night before, including a baseball, cleats, a football and a basketball.

"Wow, seriously? I guess you were right, Lucinda must be trying to give you a hint," I said, trying to lighten the mood.

"Yeah, I'm glad she thought to get me this, though," Kevin said happily, holding up a new sketch book and drawing pencils.

"That's true and those are sweeeeet," I said, dragging out the word.

"True dat," he said. "Now, open yours," he added impatiently.

"Sheesh, keep your shirt on. I'm doing it now."

My gifts were a little better than Kevin's in the respect that Lucinda got me items I could at least use. I got a makeup case filled with Elle makeup, a hairbrush set that would come in handy and a hair dryer. I set the makeup case and hair dryer to the side and opened my last two packages which turned out to be a book that I had already purchased the night before for my Kindle and a giant can filled with miniature chocolate candy bars. I was disappointed I didn't get the heat iron for my hair I asked for, but the tin of chocolates was a nice treat.

"Should take Mom her presents?" Kevin asked, munching on one of his own chocolates while I rounded up the wrapping.

"Nah, no reason to poke the sleeping beast," I joked, trying to take the abnormality out of our Christmas. "I'm gonna take out the trash, and then I'll make us some breakfast, okay?"

"Okay," he said, propping his new sketch pad up against his scrawny knees.

I pulled my hoodie on over my thermal pajama shirt and grabbed the light bag off the floor. My forward momentum out the front door was stalled from a huge gift basket sitting on the top step of the trailer. I looked around for who had left it, but saw no one. The sheer weight of the basket was more than I expected as I grunted, trying to pick it up.

"Holy Toledo, where did that come from?" Kevin asked as I staggered in.

"I don't know," I said, setting it down on the table so we could both peer inside.

"Wow, that's a pie," Kevin said, pulling an item out of the far side of the basket. "Sweet, it's cherry. Wait, is that a ham?" he asked with wide eyes as I pulled the main item out of the center of the basket.

"Yeah it is," I whispered, wondering if Old Man Wither was once again responsible for swooping in and saving the day.

"Oh my God, mashed potatoes," Kevin said, holding up a container of ready-made spuds.

"And corn and green beans," I added, handing him two more containers to add to his stack.

"And rolls," he said, holding up a package of rolls. "Oh, and presents," he said, discovering two packages at the bottom of the basket.

Now I was really confused. If Old Man Wither had given us our gifts the day before, who was the basket from?

"Katelyn, look, it's an Angry Birds t-shirt and a game for my DSI," Kevin said, holding up his loot.

Clarity instantly sank in as I looked at his gifts, feeling a mixture of both gratitude and mortification.

"Here, Katelyn, this one's yours," Kevin said, handing over a small gift-wrapped box attached to a card.

Pulling the package away from the envelope, I carefully set the gift-wrapped package on my knees while I opened the card with trembling fingers and read the contents.

Katelyn,

My family's Christmas wish was to make sure you and

Kevin had a nice meal to enjoy on Christmas Day. I know how

proud you are and like to keep your problems to yourself, but

we hope you accept this gift.

Love always, Max

P.S. A little bird mentioned to my dad that Kevin had a new DSI, which is why we bought him the game.

My heart dropped as I reread his words. Was it pride that had prevented me from allowing Max in? At the time, my actions seemed so justified, but as I rubbed my fingers over his written words my actions seemed so cold and callous.

"Katelyn, aren't you going to open your present?" Kevin asked.

"Sure, bud," I said, setting the card aside to be analyzed later. I pulled the wrapping away, taking care not to tear it.

I slowly opened the small velvet box underneath the paper and gasped when I saw the heart-shaped pendent attached to a delicate gold chain nestled inside. I pulled it gently from the box, holding it up so Kevin and I could get a better look. It swayed back and forth as I held it up, revealing an engraving on the backside.

Turning it around, I read four simple words—My Heart is Yours.

I felt an instant lump in my throat. I've never had feelings this strong for anyone before. Was it possible after only our brief time together that his feelings matched mine? I had spent the last two months burying my own feelings, thinking I was doing the right thing, but after reading the words on the back of the pendant as it swayed gently in front of my face, I felt a greater sense of longing and regret.

"That's pretty," Kevin said, breaking the trance the necklace had put me under.

"It is, isn't it," I said, clasping it around my neck.

"Max?" Kevin inquired.

I nodded. "Cool shirt," I said, looking at the slightly big shirt he had slipped over his pajamas.

"I know, right," he said, looking down at the big red bird that dominated the front of the shirt.

"Alright, how about you help me put away these goodies," I said, indicating the food that littered the top of the coffee table.

Chapter 14

The rest of our Christmas break passed with Kevin and me spending most of our time together reading and taking turns playing his DSI. Though he was practically half my age, his video game skills put mine to shame, and he giggled obsessively every time he beat me, which was nincty nine percent of the time.

The food Max's family gave us for Christmas dinner lasted several days, allowing me to stretch our other groceries and leaving me optimistic about making it until Lucinda's card got replenished.

Bethany and I hung out for a while after Christmas, but wound up fighting when she spied the heart-shaped pendant around my neck. After being put through the third degree, I finally relented and told her it was from Max. She stomped out my room in a huff after I refused her request to return it to him.

Lucinda stayed in her room the majority of the time, only emerging to use the bathroom or to tell me to pipe down when Bethany had blown a gasket. I couldn't help noticing that her skin was beginning to take on a sallow complexion from being cooped up in her small room constantly, chain-smoking. I tried to encourage her to join us in the living room, but she ignored my suggestion. The only thing she uttered, besides telling us to shut up was to not touch the remaining Christmas stuff until Jim came home. I didn't bother reminding her that Jim's public defender had told us he would most likely serve the majority of his sentence. The defender hoped to have Jim out after he served six months.

The day before school was due to start up again, we got our first eviction notice. My heart broke when I saw it. I knew I should have been expecting it considering we had been through this drill many times over the years, but I had somehow allowed myself to believe this time could be different. I showed the notice to Lucinda before crumpling it up. I wanted to keep it from Kevin, but Lucinda flew into a rant, saying it was inevitable that he would find out anyway. We had to listen as she screamed about the injustice of the situation and how grossly unfairly we were being treated. I sent Kevin to his room and continued to listen to Lucinda's tirade until she crashed into a self-medicated stupor. I left her snoring on the sofa as I headed to my room. One thing I had learned from experience is that screaming about injustice would not resolve anything. The countdown had started and in ninety days we would be escorted off the premises by the local cops.

That night I didn't sleep a wink as I tossed and turned, trying to decide how I should handle our current situation. Receiving the notice made me rethink wearing Max's necklace to school. I hated to give him false hope by wearing the token of his love when I knew we'd be leaving sooner than later.

The lack of sleep gave me a massive stress headache the next morning, making the freezing cold trudge to the bus stop even less bearable. I was tempted just to go back home and crawl into bed.

As tempting as the idea was, I got on the bus anyway, nervously playing with my necklace during the short ride to school. A bus full of screaming kids wasn't exactly the best remedy for a pounding headache. By the time we made to school, I had to take a detour to the bathroom outside of Kevin's classroom to empty the contents of my stomach.

"You okay?" Rebecca asked as I emerged from the stall.

"Yeah, I just have a stinking headache," I said, trying to smile, but felt it was closer to a grimace.

"Do you need to go home?" she asked concerned, taking in my ashen complexion.

"No, I'll be fine," I lied, not wanting to admit that I would rather have an ax to the head then listen to round two of Lucinda's rants.

"Here, how about some Advil then?" she asked, extracting a small tin of pills from her shoulder bag.

"That would be great," I said, smiling gratefully.

I washed the pills down with a bottle of water she handed me.

"Did you have a nice holiday?" she asked as we made our way to the classroom.

"Not bad, how about you?" I asked, trying to take my mind off the pain in my head.

"It was great. We went skiing in Tahoe," she said, chattering away.

I listened to her, but in sort of a half-dazed state as we entered the room. Despite the pain in my head, my eyes instantly zoned in on my first sight of Max in more than a week.

He smiled at me, glancing at the necklace I wore around my neck. I watched his smile broaden as he approached me.

"You got your gifts?" he asked as I nervously twisted it around in my fingers.

"I did," I said, losing myself in his eyes. "Thank you so much. It's beautiful," I said, grimacing from a sudden sharp pain that stabbed through my head, reminding me of its presence.

"You okay?" he asked, grabbing onto my elbow.

"Not really, my head is killing me," I answered honestly.

"Do you want me to take you home?" he asked concerned.

"No, I really don't want to go home," I mumbled.

"Did something happen?" he asked, sweeping his eyes over me looking for an injury.

"No, not this time," I said, touched by his concern. "It's just other stuff."

"Katelyn, Max, can you two find your seats?" Mr. Graves said, stepping up to the front of the classroom.

"Um, sir, Katelyn has a really bad headache. Do you think I can take her to the nurse's clinic?"

"Katelyn, do you just want to go home?" Mr. Graves asked, making him the third person in less than five minutes to ask.

"No, really," I said quietly as he approached us. "It's just, the light in here is making it worse. If I could just lie down for a little while, it will go away. I get them all the time," I added.

"Hmm, that sounds like migraines. Are you on medicine for them?"

"No, I just pop a few Advil and normally sleep them off," I mumbled, squinting my eyes to help alleviate the pain some.

"Max, why don't you escort Katelyn to the teachers' lounge instead. That light remains off the majority of the day, unlike the clinic. Grab her one of my Cokes out of the refrigerator; caffeine usually helps my wife when she gets a migraine."

Max propelled me from the room, keeping an arm firmly around my waist. I knew every eye probably followed us out of the room, but I couldn't find the energy to care. The teachers' lounge was only three rooms down from our class, but by the time we made it there, my stomach was threatening mutiny once again. Max helped me to the couch, and I gratefully sank back on the cushions.

"Here, lie down," Max said, gently nudging me back against one of the throw pillows.

"Thanks," I said, keeping my eyes closed.

A few moments later, I heard Max pulling the tab on a soda before handing it over to me. "Here you go, take a few drinks of this."

The ice-cold liquid helped ease my unfortunate nausea. "I'm going to put it here in case you need it, okay?" Max asked before heading out the door.

I nodded before sinking into blissful, headache-free sleep.

Several hours later, I woke to the door slowly opening. Blinking in the dim light, I saw Mr. Graves smiling down kindly at me. "How's the head?" he asked, sitting on the edge of the table.

"Better," I said truthfully, able to sit up. "What time is it?"

"Lunchtime," he said, handing me my lunch bag.

"Wow, seriously? I so didn't mean to sleep half the school day away."

"It's no problem, you look much better at least."

"Ha, thanks."

"I've wanted to talk to you anyway about this," he said, indicating an overflowing folder on the table next to him.

"What's that?" I asked, nibbling the corner of my sandwich.

"It's your school transcripts with feedback from all your teachers over the years."

"Really?" I asked as my curiosity piqued. I yearned to look inside it. After years of leaving my belongings behind each time we moved, the idea of having something so concrete from my past that proved I actually existed made me want to scoop the folder up and never return it. To actually have a tangible item that could be held was surreal. "What did they all have to say?" I asked, fighting the urge to see for myself.

"Well, they all agree you're a bright girl, that you're good-natured and a welcome addition to any classroom. Reading over many of the different comments, though, I see where they show extensive concern over your home life," he said gently.

I nodded my head, suddenly sick of all the pretenses. He had the proof in his hands anyway. I could only imagine the things some of my more observant teachers might have added over the years.

"It's bad?" he probed.

I nodded again.

"Do you trust me enough to tell me about it?"

I studied him for a moment, contemplating keeping my mouth closed like I always had, but before I was even aware of doing it, I allowed everything to pour out of me. I told him about the abuse, being homeless, never having enough to eat and even confided my biggest fear that Kevin would someday get caught in the line of fire. All my worries flooded out as if someone had opened up a dam. Mr. Graves sat patiently, without interrupting and when I was finally spent, he commented.

"Katelyn, you are a truly phenomenal person," he said quietly.

"No I'm not," I said, ducking my head down in embarrassment.

"Yes, you are. The things you've been through and have seen should have beaten you down, but instead you persevered, which is an admirable characteristic."

"I've only persevered for Kevin's sake," I said.

"Exactly, you put the needs and wants of your brother ahead of your own. If it wasn't for your fear of being separated, you would have reported your mom a long time ago, right?"

I nodded.

"See, there you have it. Now we just need to fix your current circumstances. I'm going to put feelers out to see if there are any local foster families that would be willing to take in siblings."

I started to protest, but he held up his hand.

"Don't worry, I'll do it discreetly," he said. "We only need to get you to eighteen, and then you can petition the courts for custody of Kevin yourself."

"We only have eighty-nine days until we're kicked out," I reminded him. "I'm not sure if Lucinda will wait to for Jim to get released when we get evicted or just move on. Truthfully, I'm surprised she's still sticking around and hasn't moved us yet."

"Will she let you know ahead of time?" he asked, sharing my concern.

"She never has before. Normally, it's a one-day notice, sometimes less. When we lived in Texas, she woke Kevin and me up after we had only been sleeping for an hour and told us to pack a bag because we were leaving. Most times it was to skip out on rent or bounced checks or something, but it could have been because of that too," I said, indicating the folder. "Only she knows the real reasons for the hasty moves we've made, all I can do is guess."

He looked disgusted at my words. "So she skips out instead of facing the music," he said.

"Yep, that sounds about right."

"Alright," he said, taking a deep breath. "So we know time is of the essence. I'm going to go home and talk to my wife about applying for foster status. Our kids are all living their own lives now, leaving just my wife and me to rattle around our big house by ourselves. Would you be okay with that?"

I nodded, not daring to believe he was serious. "Until I turn eighteen," I said, trying to reassure him that he wouldn't be stuck with us forever.

"For as long as you need us," he corrected, making my heart swell.

"Okay, so you'll ask your wife?" I asked, expecting several roadblocks that could derail his generous offer.

"I believe that will be more of a formality," he said, smiling at me.

"Then I'll keep my fingers crossed," I said pessimistically. He meant well, but in all honesty, things like this never worked out for Kevin and me.

"Katelyn, we'll work this out. I promise."

"I don't know. This town is starting to feel like the 'Stepford Town.' Everyone is just way too nice," I said, trying to remove some of the pressure off of him.

He laughed. "Being nice isn't a bad thing. Do you feel good enough to return to class?"

"Yeah, my headache is all but gone," I said, standing up.

Max was just finishing up his lunch when we returned to the classroom. His eyes met mine and I returned a thankful look. I knew I was probably opening myself up for a major letdown, but I decided in that moment I no longer cared. My face must have given Max some kind of indication as to what I was thinking because he grinned widely and waved me over to him.

"I moved your desk back. Is that okay?"

"That's perfect," I answered, looking at Bethany who was obviously fuming. I didn't like hurting her feelings, but I had spent the past two months trying to convince myself that I was just like her because we both came from nothing. The truth is that being poor is the only thing we had in common. Unlike Bethany, I didn't blame the rest of the world for my problems. Life was tough enough without carrying around that kind of hate. For her sake, I hope she gets over that one day.

Max squeezed my hand lightly as I slid into my seat. "Thanks for the necklace and the rest of the stuff," I whispered as Mr. Graves started covering the different layers of an atom.

The rest of the day passed in a happy blur. Every once in a while Max would reach over to touch me as if he was reassuring himself I wouldn't leave.

***

The days following my reconciliation with Max were the happiest of my life. Kevin and I spent most our afternoons at Max's large and inviting home. His parents took to Kevin immediately and I watched him blossom under their affection and attentiveness. I put aside my embarrassment over the Halloween fiasco and the fool Lucinda had made of herself in the grocery store with Max's dad. Kevin and I were invited to dinner every night, and at first I felt bad for the imposition, but I quickly began to realize they seemed to enjoy our company.

The free meals took the pressure off of worrying about Lucinda's welfare card which was a good thing since the January money was spent much like the December money had been. Lucinda used the small amount of cash she acquired to pay for gas to visit Jim and purchase more cigarettes. If not for Max's parents, Kevin and I would have surely starved. I was unsure of how she was surviving, but I did notice that many nights she slept elsewhere, leaving the trailer to Kevin and me. She was uncommunicative when I tried to press for details, choosing to either outright ignore me or give me a slap for annoying her.

As January crept into February, Kevin and I were only home at night and as little as possible on the weekends. He

240

quickly became the mascot for our group and hung out with us the majority of the time. Lucinda's erratic behavior kept me from wanting to leave him with her, and Max seemed to know this without a word from me. Though he did grumble about what an excellent chaperone Kevin made for us. I laughed at his complaints, but felt the same frustration at times, especially when our heated kisses began to escalate, only to crash down to reality when Kevin would give us an "ew, gross." Needless to say, it was a definite mood killer once he piped in.

I was over at Max's house the week before Valentine's Day when he asked if I was comfortable enough leaving Kevin with his parents while we went out for Valentine's Day. We had snuck down the hall to the movie room to get a few minutes by ourselves.

"Don't they want to go out themselves?" I asked, standing by the recliner he had sunk into while I munched on a licorice whip.

"Nah, my dad says it gives him an excuse to stay home instead of fighting for a table with a bunch of lovesick couples," Max reassured me, laughing. "Besides, they plan on getting that new movie he and Kevin have been itching to see on Netflix."

"Your parents have been really great," I said, letting him pull me on to his lap.

"Where's the kissing police?" he asked, nuzzling his lips into my neck, making me shiver in anticipation.

"Mmm, that feels good," I said as I leaned my head back to give him better access. "He's in the kitchen with your mom," I said, distracted when he dragged my lips to his. I opened my mouth and tangled my tongue with his, making him groan this time. "I love you," I added through a half moan in the heat of the moment. I came crashing back to Earth when he stopped kissing me. I looked at him with vulnerable eyes, wondering how he would react. The words had just slipped out of nowhere. The only other person I had uttered them to in years had been Kevin, but I had known for several weeks that I was in love with Max.

I waited with baited breath for his response as we continued to stare deep into each other's eyes. "You do?" he finally choked out.

I nodded. "Look, I know it might be too soon and I shouldn't..." I said until my voice trailed off as he crushed his lips to mine.

"I love you too," he said, pulling back after a moment. "I think I've loved you for months. I've never believed in love at first sight, but I do believe in fate. Every crappy situation you've had to overcome led you here. I've never felt this way about anyone, and it's because I've been waiting for you, I just didn't know it until you got here."

"I think so too," I said, feeling my heart melt at his words of confirmation. I pulled him back to me, tangling my fingers through his lush auburn hair. He settled firmly against my body by placing his hands on my hips. I could feel his passion matching mine and I moaned again as his hands sought the firm skin of my stomach, slowly inching up my midriff. I shifted my hips more, snuggling against him and making him well aware of how I was feeling. Liquid fire poured through my veins as I strained even closer. His needs matched my own and I felt his hand creep farther up until it rested right below my bra. I fought the urge to beg him to continue and deepened the kiss even further. He sensed my desire and moved his hand further up, resting it finally where I wanted it the most. The moment was ours as his hand explored my body, causing me to gasp with pleasure.

"I think they're in the movie room waiting for us," I heard Max's dad say in a voice that sounded like it was coming through a tunnel.

Max's hand retreated at his words and I wanted to cry out in frustration. Giving my lips one last nip, he shifted me off his lap in one deft movement. I gripped the arm of the La-Z-Boy, trying to get my racing heart beat back to normal.

"Yep, I was right, they were kissing," Kevin said, trailing behind Maxwell and Karen.

"Hush, Kevin," Karen said, chastising Kevin good-naturedly. "You'll embarrass your sister. I'm sure they were in here discussing a homework assignment or something to that effect," she added, grinning at me mischievously.

243

"Um, yeah, that's right," I said, slightly flustered. His parents were cool for the most part, but I was pretty sure their trust in us would be put to the test if they saw how close we had come to removing our clothes just a few moments ago.

Max grinned at me sheepishly, obviously guessing what my beat red face indicated. He playfully grabbed at me as we settled onto the oversized bean bag chair.

"Behave," I said out of the corner of my mouth. "Or I'll have to go sit with Kevin," I threatened.

"Hmm, okay, but you'd be sitting with my parents too," he chided quietly.

I turned around to see that Kevin had made himself right at home between Maxwell and Karen on the full-size couch that sat on the other side of the room. Normally, he preferred to sit on the humongous navy blue bean bag chair closest to the big screen television, but looking at him sandwiched between Max's parents, he looked quite content. In an alternant universe, this would have been Kevin's life, surrounded by people who loved him. I smiled happily and felt my new love for Max's family overflowing in me. Whatever happened in the future, at least Kevin and I were happy at this very moment.

Chapter 15

The following weekend Max and I headed to Bozeman, leaving Kevin behind with Karen and Maxwell, which worked out well since Lucinda had been MIA most of the week.

"Sooo, where are going?" I asked for the hundredth time as Max accelerated toward the bigger city.

"Now if I told you, it would ruin the surprise," he said, pretending to sigh heavily.

"Surprise, smurprise," I said, grumbling good-naturedly.

Max shot me his dimpled grin. I leaned over and pressed my lips to the small little sunk-in space on his face. He rested his hand on my knee and gave it a light squeeze. "Are you trying to make us wreck," he said huskily.

"No," I said, sliding back to my seat. "I've just wanted to do that for months," I added.

"Really?" he asked, grinning widely.

"Don't let it go to your head. I feel that way about most dimples I see," I said.

"Oh yeah? Well, my grandpa looks just like me, dimples and all. Will I have to keep you two separated?" he teased, winking at me.

"Funny, you just might," I said, feeling a sudden pang of envy that he had so many people who loved him. Lucinda never talked much about her parents, and I had never met them. My life had been made up of a long line of strangers who floated out of our lives as quickly as they had entered it. When she tried, Lucinda could be very engaging and once she laid out her sob story about never getting a decent break, most people were more than willing to lend a helping hand. Unfortunately, it didn't take long for Lucinda to bite that helping hand and show her true colors. After a while, I stopped allowing myself to get close to anyone, knowing in the end they only would wind up hating us when we screwed them over one way or another. Lucinda had burned so many bridges over the years by scamming people that retaining friendships was obsolete.

"Hey, why the sudden long face?" Max asked concerned.

"Huh?" I asked, coming back to reality. "It's nothing, I was just thinking."

"About what?"

"Just how different our lives have been," I answered honestly. "You've never had to move and you're surrounded by grandparents, aunts, uncles and cousins galore. Don't our differences bother you sometimes?" I asked, tugging on my bottom lip.

"Katelyn, you couldn't be further from the truth. The only thing that bothers me is the shit you've had to put up with. I know talking about your mom is a taboo subject, but the thought of her hurting one hair on your head is enough to make me want to pound something. I've never been the violent type, but when it comes to you, I go nuts."

"I'm sure there's millions of kids who have had it worse than me. Matter of fact, I've met several of them over the years. Plenty have wound up in the hospital after being abused or neglected."

"I'm sure you've had lots of times where you probably should have gone to the hospital too," he said, looking at my head meaningfully.

I touched the spot Old Man Wither had fixed up for me self-consciously. "Maybe," I said, feeling slightly betrayed that Wither had given away my secret.

"He only told my dad," Max said, sensing the betrayal I felt. "He knows my uncle is a lawyer and wanted to see if there was any way to help you and Kevin without getting social services involved."

I gasped at the thought of the Department of Children and Families getting involved.

"It's fine," Max said, patting my knee. "Old Man Wither made my dad and uncle promise not to do anything. He knows you don't want to lose Kevin, and he seems to really care about you two a lot."

"He's definitely a cool guy," I said, relieved that he had stuck to his word. "I feel awful that he and his wife never had kids. I think it's ironic how people that want children so badly are denied, but those that should have never been able to reproduce have no problem doing it."

"I agree, it's messed up. I definitely hate your mom, but I can't help wondering if I would have met you now if she wasn't so wacked-out."

"I thought you believe in fate," I said laughing, trying to steer the conversation away from the doom and gloom I had dragged it into.

"Oh, believe me, I do. I'm just saying, how much would it suck to have to wait several more years to meet the woman I love?"

"Hmmm, I like the sound of that," I said, laying my head on his shoulder as we neared the city.

Max deftly maneuvered the SUV through the streets that seemed insanely congested after the limited traffic we were used to. After a few moments, he pulled into a parking spot in front of a large glass and brick building. A sign off to the side welcomed us to the Bozeman Public Library.

"We're going to the library?" I asked excitedly.

"Yeah, I remember you mentioning once that the happiest moments of your life were spent in libraries with all the books. I just figured I wanted in on the happiest moments of your life too," he said, lacing his fingers through mine.

I paused in the middle of the sidewalk as a light snow began to fall on us. "Silly boy, you surpassed those memories long ago," I said, placing my cold lips on his.

"So you mean this'll be like a grand slam?" He gently teased, leading me out of the cold into the warm interior of the building.

I laughed. "Most definitely," I said, taking in my surroundings. "I wish we could get a library card," I added wistfully, looking at the endless rows of books. "I know I have my Kindle, but look at all these books," I said, sweeping out my arms to indicate the overflowing shelves.

"Yeah, the commute makes that tough, but are you ready for part two of your Valentine's Day surprise?"

"Part two? How many parts are there?"

"That's for me to know and you to find out," he said, giving my bottom a light pat as we headed toward the back of the library where several rooms lined the far wall. He steered me toward one that had a sign proclaiming *used books for sale*. "I bought you a twenty-dollar gift card and each book is only fifty cents, so let's see what kind of damage you can do," he said, winking at me.

"I get to pick out forty books?" I laughed, feeling giddy as I headed toward my favorite genre. "It'll be a shame to leave them behind when I move, but..." I said, letting my voice trail off at the now sour look on his face. He hated when I mentioned the pending move, but I wanted to keep us firmly rooted in reality. We had already stayed in Four Corners longer than any other place, and the ticking eviction clock was already at the halfway mark.

"You won't have to leave them behind," he said stubbornly.

"Okay," I said, trying to appease him so I wouldn't ruin the perfect date he had planned. I knew there was still a remote possibility that we would get to stay since Mr. Graves was still diligently trying to cut through the red tape to become a temporary foster parent.

Max let the subject drop and after a few moments of silence he got into the game of trying to help me fill my quota of books.

"How about this one?" he asked, holding up yet another sci-fi book.

"Ha ha, you're such a crack-up," I said, socking his arm lightly.

"What?" he asked, feigning innocence.

"If it doesn't have hot guys and kissing, I'm out," I said teasingly.

"What hot guys?" He mock growled, making a grab for me.

"You know, tall, dreamy, dark hair, drop-dead gorgeous eyes and..." my words were cutoff as his lips claimed mine. "And dimples that make your toes curl," I added breathlessly.

"Hmmm, toes curl, that's hot," he said, nipping on the corner of my mouth. "How many books are you up to?"

I looked down at the stacks of books around our ankles. "I think I'm two away," I said, grabbing two random books from the shelf as he distracted me by gently blowing on the hair at the back of my neck. "You're going to get us kicked out," I added, shooting a look at the elderly gentleman who was manning the small register by the door.

"You mean to tell me all those times you spent in the library over the years you never thought about making out?" he whispered in my ear as his teeth grazed the lobe.

I blushed at his words because I had indeed fantasized about such a situation.

"Come on, time for part three of your Valentine's Day surprise," he said, grabbing up two stacks of books to carry up to the counter. I followed behind, carrying one of the other stacks in my arm as he came back for the remaining books. The old man behind the counter gave us a knowing look over his spectacles as Max kept his arms firmly wrapped around me from behind.

"We'll come back and get these in a little while," Max told him.

"That's fine, I'll hold your bags here," he said, placing them on the back counter behind him.

"Are we leaving the library and coming back?" I asked, feeling remorseful at having to leave my books behind. I was worried the library would close while we were gone eating dinner.

"Nope, we're staying here," Max said, dragging me back up to the front of the library. He veered off to the left instead of heading out the front doors, leading me down a brightly-lit hallway that opened up into a small café called Lindley Perk Coffee Shop.

"We're eating here?" I asked happily, studying the small menu board.

"Well, not in here, but back there," he said, jerking a thumb back the way we had come.

"Um, I'm pretty sure they won't let us bring food and drinks into the actual library," I said, hating to burst his bubble and ruin his surprise.

"Actually we can," he said, pointing to a sign behind the counter encouraging patrons to *feel free to browse the book shelves with their food in hand.*

"Seriously? Oh my God, that's awesome."

"I thought you'd like that," he said, lacing his fingers through mine as we approached the counter. "I called ahead," he told the clerk when she asked for our order.

"Name?" she asked, chomping on a piece of gum.

"Maxwell Jr."

"You called an order in for us?" I asked, touched at his thoughtfulness.

"I had to make sure my plans were going to work out," he said, paying the salesclerk.

"Well aren't you debonair," I said as the salesclerk handed over a white bag with our food and two large cups of steaming latte.

"GQ-smooth baby," he said, shooting me a cocky grin.

"That's true, you're as smooth as a baby's bottom," I teased.

"Ugh, there's no baby here," he said, making a show of flexing his muscles.

I giggled as we weaved through the endless shelves of books throughout the library. An elderly woman frowned at me and made a production of shushing me.

"Oops, sorry," I mouthed as Max continued to drag me to a lone table in the far corner of the library.

We ate our sandwiches and chips, talking quietly in between bites. It was by far the most romantic date I had ever gone on, and I told him so. "Well, it's not over yet," he said, pulling out a small wrapped package.

"You already got me a gift," I protested.

"This is surprise number four," he said, smiling nervously at me.

Apprehension filled me as I pulled off the wrapping paper to reveal a small jewelry box. Lifting the lid, I gasped when I saw the diamond-encrusted interlocking heart ring inside. My stomach dropped, and I looked up at him in confusion.

"It's not an engagement ring," he said quickly as I let out a relieved pent-up breath. "It's a promise ring."

"Oh Max, that's sweet," I said, pulling the ring out.

"Some guys use it as a kind of 'I promise to eventually marry you' thing, but I didn't get yours for that," he said. "Mine stands for something else," he added quietly.

"What does it stand for?" I asked as he laced his finger through mine.

"It stands for all the promises I intend to keep to you. I promise to protect you from any more harm, and I promise I will do everything in my power to make sure you get your 'someday soon.'"

"How did you find out about someday soon?" I asked, already knowing the answer.

"Kevin made a comment to my mom and dad about it last week when he was helping them bake cookies in the kitchen."

"What did he say?" I asked, feeling my heart swell painfully.

"He asked them if this was what someday soon would be like. They were confused at first until he filled them in."

"Oh," I said, looking down. "I bet they thought it was ridiculous for a seventeen-year-old to make such promises."

"Actually, they thought how incredibly brave it was," he said, lifting my chin to meet his eyes.

He leaned over and pressed his lips to mine. I closed my eyes, relishing in the sensation of so much love flowing through me.

"How about we get out of here?" he asked against my lips as a librarian wheeled an overflowing book cart down the row near us.

"Sounds good," I said, gathering up our trash after sliding the elegant ring onto my right hand.

"It's lovely," I said, giving him a quick peck on the mouth after admiring it on my hand.

"It suits you," he said.

Max grabbed the heavy bags with my books from the elderly gentleman and we slipped and slid our way to the SUV on the now slick sidewalk.

"I'm not sure I'll ever get used to this weather," I complained, blowing on my cold fingers.

"You'll get used to it, and just wait until summertime is here. We usually stay outside the majority of the day."

"I can't wait," I said, still shivering as Max got back out of the vehicle to scrape the ice from the windshield.

"When does summer start around here?" I joked as he joined me several minutes later, shivering too.

"Not soon enough," he said laughing as I cranked the heat up even warmer and switched on my seat warmer. "You just lack proper threads," he teased, looking down at my naked hands.

"Yeah, I know," I said, looking down at my red wind-chapped fingers.

Max turned on the radio and switched it to a station playing current hits. He sang along with the lyrics while I watched admiringly. "Pretty bad, huh?" he asked, several songs later.

"Well, it's better than a bullfrog," I teased.

"Gee, thanks."

"Kidding," I giggled. "You sound great, though I do find it insane that you know all the words to every song."

"It's a given to know all the words, they play the same songs over and over again. Don't you listen to music?" he asked.

"Sure, whenever we have a car that has a working radio in it, but it's usually never current stuff. Lucinda's a stickler about the music she'll listen to."

"Seems like she's a stickler about a lot of things," he grumbled under his breath.

"You get used to it," I said indifferently.

"Yeah, but most parents aren't like that," he said testily.

"I know," I said, wondering why he was trying to pick a fight.

"If she's so goddamn awful, why do you always defend her?"

"I don't defend her," I said defensively. "Why the hell are we even discussing this?" I asked, starting to get angry over his mood swing. "Everything was fine back in the library."

Max turned off the main road onto a small snow-covered dirt road abruptly making the vehicle bounce around uncomfortably. After a few moments, we were surrounded by trees as the road behind us disappeared from sight.

Max undid his seatbelt and used the automatic switch to move his seat as far back as it would go so he could better face me. "I just don't want to lose you," he finally said.

"I'll come back," I said quietly.

"What if something comes up? What if you meet someone else, or God forbid, your mom actually kills you on one of her rants."

"Don't be silly, I'm not going to meet anyone else, and Lucinda's rants never go that far."

"Katelyn, don't treat me like I'm stupid. She bashed your head in with who knows what a couple months ago."

"A coffee mug," I said simply.

He reached over and undid my seatbelt. With one swift movement he had me across the center console and onto his lap. The wide seats of the SUV allowed me to straddle him without much discomfort.

"How can I keep my promise to protect you if you won't let anyone report her?"

"You just have to trust me," I said, resting my forehead against his.

"I trust you. It's her I don't trust," he said, running his hands through my hair before dragging my lips to his. "Do you understand how tough this is and how much you mean to me?" He asked raggedly once our lips parted.

I nodded my head. His pain was tangible and my heart ached in my inability to ease it. "What can I do?" I asked, desperate to sooth the pain he was going through.

"Stop her before it's too late," he begged.

"Anything but that," I pleaded.

"Please," he said before crushing his lips to mine. His searing kiss sparked a fire throughout my entire body. He dug his hands under my multiple layers of clothing until they found the skin they sought. I approved with pleasure as his hands moved at their own accord up over my ribcage. I could feel his need beneath me as I shifted closer, trying to consume as much of him as possible. His hands reached around behind me and fumbled with the clasp on my bra. I knew I should halt things before they could get any further out of control, but I couldn't remember any of my reasons for waiting. Reaching up behind me, I released the clasp for him and sighed in relief when his hands finally found what they yearned for. Max's tongue plunged deeper into my mouth as I moved against him, burning with desire. I pulled at his clothing, desperate to touch the skin beneath them. He dragged his lips and hand from me and ripped off his jacket and sweater, leaving his rock-hard chest naked in front of me. I ran my hands up over his stomach and chest, loving the way the muscles rippled beneath my fingertips. I leaned forward, sliding my tongue over his collarbone, making him moan. I smiled at his response, trailing my tongue up over his chin until I reached his lips. He rested his hands on my hips as I devoured his mouth and then slowly moved them to the hem of my clothes and started to peal the multiple layers from me. I shivered as he pulled my hoodie away leaving behind only my thin t-shirt. I pulled back and met his questioning eyes, nodding my approval as he slowly lifted my shirt upward.

The ringing of his phone broke the moment and he fumbled for his iPhone in the center console next to me.

"Yeah?" He said in his usual way of answering his phone. "Oh, hey Mom," he said, and I instantly came back to my senses as I heard her tell him Kevin was sick. I swung off his lap and into my own seat. "Okay, we were on our way home already, we should be there in fifteen minutes," he said. His mom talked for several more seconds. "I'll ask her," he said, looking at me. "My mom said Kevin is running a fever and she wants to know if she can set you guys up in the guest room so you don't have to drag him back out in the snow." I nodded my approval. "She says that's fine, Mom. Okay, we'll be there in a few minutes," he said before hanging up.

"Wow, Kevin takes his chaperone duties seriously," Max joked as he started the vehicle and pulled his sweater back on.

I burst out laughing, fixing the last of my clothing. "True dat," I said in typical Kevin fashion. "You sure your parents don't mind us staying over?"

"Are you kidding? She's worried Kevin has a fever, but I could tell she was thrilled you guys are staying over. My mom loves having company over. As a matter fact, so do I," he said, raising his eyebrows at me suggestively.

"Hmm, looks like I'll be locking my door tonight," I said now that I had come back to my senses. "I don't think having unprotected sex is something that would improve my current situation," I said truthfully.

"What makes you think I wasn't prepared?" he asked.

"Were you?" I asked as my heart skipped several beats.

He nodded. "Does that bother you?"

"I don't know. I always said I would wait since Lucinda was so promiscuous, but things look a little different now. I do know I don't want to rush into it though," I added, trying to express the mixed-up feelings I was having.

"So, we take things slow," he said, lacing his fingers through mine. "Like maybe alone time in the car should be limited," he quipped.

"Um yeah, I'd have to agree with you there," I said giggling. "I think it's the leather seats, they make us act like love-starved maniacs," I said, flushing slightly as I recalled how intimately his hands had touched me just moment before.

Chapter 16

Taking things slow proved to be more of a challenge than we could have ever imagined as February faded away and March began. Even with Kevin acting as a chaperone, the air around us seemed to sizzle from the need we both acutely felt. We planned our dates in group settings to help us both behave, but that only proved to frustrate us further since even our chaste kisses made me ache. I knew Max was suffering as much as I was with the constant smoldering looks he shot my way, making it impossible to think of anything else but his lips and hands on me.

School at least helped to some degree as we prepared for SATs and our college applications. Mr. Graves and the other teachers stepped in to help me pull my transcripts together so I would at least be eligible to apply to a community college, wherever I might be. Mr. Graves remained optimistic about getting approved to become foster parents before Lucinda could move us, so he encouraged me to check out the community college in Bozeman. Max was applying to the University of Montana in Bozeman, so I grudgingly agreed, even though I still felt a long way off from being ready for any kind of college. Max and I took Kevin with us to check out the campuses on his birthday, March twentieth. We planned to take him to a local comic book store and out to eat once we were done.

Max and Kevin hung out together while I met with a counselor at the school. By the time we met back up, I was loaded down with forms and school catalogs the friendly woman had given me.

"So, how did it go?" Max asked, giving me a quick peck on the lips in front of Kevin's eagle eyes.

"She said she felt I'd have no problem keeping up with college classes," I said happily, sliding my arm around his waist as we headed toward the parking lot.

"See, told you. Piece of cake."

"Well, I'm still uber nervous, but if I study hard, maybe I'll make it," I said, still not overly confident.

"Babe, you got mad skills. You've just never had the chance to fine-tune them," he said.

"Hey, you say that to me," Kevin piped in.

"Yeah I do, punk," I said, ruffling his hair. "Now it's time for some birthday fun. I have a hard-earned twenty-dollar bill with your name on it," I said, grateful to finally have money to my name. I had been working afternoons at Max's dad's store, doing what Max used to do while his dad began to train him in management. Karen stepped in and volunteered to pick Kevin up each afternoon while I worked since most evenings we were at their house for dinner anyway. The new arrangement worked out perfectly since Max and I could drive to work together. I was a little apprehensive he would get sick of me, but he seemed to crave my company as much I did his.

"And I plan on matching that twenty," Max said, reaching in his wallet to pull out a twenty.

Kevin's eyes went wide with shock as we both handed him his birthday money. "Seriously?" he asked, not daring to believe his good fortune.

"Seriously," we said in unison.

Kevin spent more than an hour at the comic book store as he happily pawed through endless cartons, looking for just the right comics. His head was already buried into one of the comics as we pulled out of the parking lot.

"So, what would you guys like for lunch?" Max asked, maneuvering out of the crowded parking lot.

"McDonald's is good," I said, looking back at Kevin. "Right bud?" I asked.

"Can we go someplace where we get served?" he asked hopefully.

"Of course we can," Max said, making a left at the light. "I know the perfect place. My parents used to take me there for my birthday."

Max took us to a swanky place called Starky's. It was packed when we arrived, but the wait line moved fast and before we knew it we were shown to a table. The décor of the restaurant was simple, but had an elegant look to it. I instantly felt out of my element, looking around at the well-dressed people around us as we made our way to our table. A string quartet played their instruments quietly on the far end of the room and many of the male diners wore suits and the women wore trendy skirts and dresses. I felt underdressed in my worn jeans and hooded sweatshirt. I opened my menu and gulped uncomfortably when I saw the higher prices.

"You okay?" Max asked as I took a nervous drink of my water.

"Yeah, I think this is a little nicer than what Kevin wanted," I said, hoping he would suggest we try somewhere else.

"No way, this is perfect," traitorous Kevin said, taking in our surroundings.

I shot a glare his way, but he was oblivious to it as he resumed reading the comic he had carried in.

"Katelyn, it's good. Okay?" Max asked, reaching for my hand.

"Ugh, how do you know me so well?" I grumbled, searching the menu for the cheapest item. *Sheesh, even the burgers are pricey. Where's the ninety-nine cent menu?* I thought to myself.

"Okay, you're over thinking this," Max said, plucking the menu from my hand. "I'll order for you. The burgers here are as close to heaven as you can get."

"Okay, a burger sounds good," I admitted grudgingly.

Max quickly took my mind off of how out of place I felt and soon we were laughing and joking around with Kevin. The meal was every bit as good as Max promised and we all dug in with gusto.

"Can we go to your house now?" Kevin asked Max as we piled into the vehicle.

"No, bud, Mom's expecting us home tonight," I said, reminding him. Lucinda had been spending a little more time at the trailer over the last few days. Her antsy behavior had me on edge, but I had kept my lips sealed around Max, knowing he would take it as a bad sign.

"Oh yeah," Kevin mumbled. "Do you think she remembered it's my birthday?" he asked sullenly.

"I'm sure she did, bud," I said, avoiding Max's eyes since he knew that I was the one responsible for reminding her.

"And don't forget, we're celebrating with my parents tomorrow night when they get back into town," Max said, looking in the rearview mirror at him.

"Yay, I forgot about that," Kevin said, easily pacified.

Max dropped us off outside our trailer just as dusk was settling in. I promised to call him later that night before closing the door behind me. Lucinda was waiting for us as soon as we entered the trailer and I knew instantly our time here was over.

My time with Max had ended.

"What's up?" I asked, trying to ignore the duffle bags waiting by the front door.

"We're leaving," Lucinda said giddily.

"Why? Did Jim get released from jail early?" I asked, grasping at straws.

"No, but things have been over between us for a while. I've met the most fabulous man you've ever laid eyes on."

My heart dropped at her words. She had already met someone else. I looked toward her room, expecting her newest infatuation to walk out. "He's not here. We're picking him up. He has to check in with his parole officer one last time, and then we'll be home free."

"Parole?" I asked.

"Yeah, it's no big deal. He did a few years for some bogus drug charge," she said unconcerned.

"I'm not ready to leave," I said sinking down on the couch.

"Aw, come on, Katelyn, you say that every time. Don't you want to know where we're going?" she asked.

I shook my head no, fighting the tears I was trying to hold back.

"Well, Ms. Negativity, we're moving to Florida. Jack has some buddies down near Miami that are going to set him up with a job. Just think, no more jackets or boots, we'll get to wear flip flops and swimsuits every day."

"I don't want to wear a swimsuit every day," Kevin piped in, still standing by the door. "I don't want to leave either. I want to stay here with Max and his parents," he added, running to his room.

"This is your fault, you selfish bitch!" Lucinda screamed at me. "You had to drag him around those people, making him believe he could fit in. Don't think I haven't noticed that ring on your finger and the gifts that boy has been buying you. He wants one thing, to get in your pants. Once you spread your legs for him, he'll be through with you."

"You're wrong, he loves me!" I yelled, standing up to face, her shaking with rage. "And his parents love us more than you ever have. Just because guys leave you after you spread your legs doesn't mean the same will happen to me," I said meanly.

She lashed out at me with the back of her hand, knocking me back onto the sofa. "You have no idea what you're talking about little girl," she snarled, towering over me. "The only reason I've been dumped is because of you two."

"Whatever helps you sleep at night," I said, making a move to stand up again.

"Fuck you!" she said, reaching out to knock me down again when a crash on the coffee table startled us.

Looking over, I saw Kevin standing with his baseball bat in hand. "Don't touch her again," he said in a wobbly voice, holding the bat with shaking hands. "We'll go with you, but you can't hit Katelyn ever again. Understand?" he said, not lowering the bat.

"Fine, I was done with her anyway. Pack your crap, we're leaving in the morning," she said, stomping down to her room.

Kevin dropped his bat and rushed to my arms. "Are you okay?" he asked with tears streaking down his cheek.

"I'm fine, bud. You didn't have to do that," I said, wrapping my arms around his shaking body.

"Yes I did. I'm the man of this family and it's my job to protect you," he said through quivering lips before he burst out in tears.

I held him while he sobbed in my arms, feeling heartsick that he had to stand up for me. Eventually his sobs died, away and he fell into an exhausted sleep. I pulled the blanket off the back of the couch and covered him. Heading toward the phone, I dialed Max's number.

"Hey you," Max said answering the phone.

His words made my mouth dry out as my heartache griped me.

"Katelyn, are you okay?" Max said anxiously.

"No," I finally said.

"I'm on my way," he said disconnecting, not needing an explanation.

I was already waiting for him outside when he screeched to a stop in front of the trailer.

"What happened?" he asked, making a move toward the trailer door.

"We're leaving tomorrow," I said, stopping him in his tracks.

"What?" he asked.

"Can we go for a drive?" I asked in a dead voice.

"Kevin?" he asked.

"He'll be fine for now. He's sleeping." I said, climbing into the SUV.

"Tell me everything," Max said, climbing into the driver's seat.

"Lucinda met someone else. Some drug dealer I think, since she said he just finished parole."

"Where does she plan on going?"

"Miami," I said.

"We can fix this. My dad can have my uncle hustle on the fostering papers for the Graves first thing Monday morning."

"It'll be too late. We leave in the morning."

"Stay with me. You'll be eighteen in six months."

"I can't. I can't abandon Kevin."

"You could report her and take your chances. At least you'd still be in this state."

"At what cost?" I asked. "Should I put Kevin's happiness above my own? What if his foster parents turn out to be assholes? What if they never let me see him?" I demanded.

"I don't know," he said, pounding the steering wheel in frustration.

"I know," I said quietly, and that was the truth. I would leave in the morning with Lucinda because Kevin had to come first. We only had to make it six months before I was an adult and able to finally make decisions. "I'll come back," I promised as a lone tear tracked down his cheek.

He pulled the vehicle down the same dirt path we had been on before and I unbuckled my seatbelt. I willingly let him pull me into his arms as he kissed me tenderly. I cupped his face and kissed the trail the lone tear had left behind. "I will come back," I said again before capturing his lips with mine. I intended the kiss to be comforting, but somewhere in the midst of the passion we had been keeping at bay things heated up. His lips claimed mine more savagely as he drank from them like a man dying of thirst. I returned his need, equally and frantically pulling at his sweater so I could run my hands over the hard planes of his body. He ripped away the clothing that was obstructing me, allowing me easy access to his warm skin. My shirt and hoodie quickly followed as we allowed ourselves to get lost in each other's bodies.

The only regret I had when we finished was that I had wasted so much time making us wait. We righted our clothing and Max slowly backed out of our hidden spot. "I will always love you," he said, looking at me long and hard before pulling onto the main road.

"And I love you too," I said sadly, clasping his hand tightly in mine.

We were almost back to the trailer park when several cop cars and an ambulance came zooming up behind us with sirens wailing. Max pulled off to the shoulder and I looked at him anxiously when the trio of emergency vehicles turned into Shady Lane. Max turned in after them and my heart dropped to my knees when I saw the vehicles screech to a stop in front of my trailer.

I didn't allow Max to fully throw the vehicle into park before I propelled myself out of my seat. In a fog, I watched as two of the cops hauled Lucinda out of the trailer as she screamed at them. "It was an accident," she screeched. "Do you really think I would hurt my little boy?"

"This is your fault," she screamed, finally spotting me. "He wouldn't leave without you! He wouldn't leave without you!" She repeated as they tossed her in the backseat of one of the cruisers. Her screams were muted, but her words ran through my head as I raced for the steps of the trailer only to be detained by one of the cops.

"You can't go in there," he said as I fought against him.

"I have to. He's my brother. He's all I have!" I yelled. "Please," I begged.

"The paramedics are trying to save him, you'll just be in the way," the cop said, relinquishing me to Max's arms.

"Please don't let him die!" I pleaded with Max.

"It'll be okay," he said, rubbing my back. "Here they come," he said as three paramedics lifted a stretcher out of the trailer.

I rushed to the stretcher as they opened the wheels underneath it. My heart stopped as I saw Kevin, hardly recognizable and covered in bruises and tubes. I reached for his hand and held it tightly in my own as they prepared to load him in the back of the ambulance.

One of the paramedics tried to make me stay behind as I followed the stretcher. "He's my brother," I gasped. "He's all I have," I added brokenly as she finally let me climb into the back of the ambulance.

"Sit there," she said, pointing to the bench seat along the side of the ambulance.

I nodded my head, feeling completely numb inside as they worked frantically over Kevin's lifeless body. I prayed silently to a God that I feared had abandoned us so many years ago as they stripped my brother's shirt away to use metal paddles on his chest. I covered my mouth in horror when I saw the black bruises covering his small precious torso.

"We're losing him," were the last words I heard before darkness took over my vision.

Chapter 17

I woke to my eyes being pried open and a bright light shining in them. Reality crashed in and I sat up abruptly.

"Whoa, take it easy," the same paramedic from earlier said as she tried to push me back down.

I resisted her shove. "Where's my brother?" I asked frantically, looking around the curtained off cubicle I was in.

"They took him to surgery," she said somberly.

"Surgery?" I squeaked. "Why?"

"I can't say. A doctor will be in to see you soon."

"Please, you have to tell me," I begged, remembering the words I heard before I passed out. "Is he dead?" I asked frantically.

"No, but he's in critical condition. His heart stopped beating in the ambulance, but we were able to get it going again," she said, sighing heavily.

"I don't want to lose him," I whispered.

"I know, honey," she said, patting my knee. "There's an anxious young man pacing the hallways waiting to see you. Can I let him in?"

"Max?" I asked, relieved I wouldn't be alone.

"I think that's what he said his name was," she said, heading out of my curtained off area.

Mere seconds passed before Max was by my side. He pulled me into his strong comforting arms as I sobbed against his chest.

"He's going to make it," Max said forcibly. I couldn't tell if he was trying to reassure me or himself.

The next few hours passed in a pain-filled blur as Max's parents arrived along with the Graves and several other adults I hadn't met. I was passed from one set of arms to another as each person shared in my grief while we waited for any kind of news.

Kevin had been in surgery for two hours when a cop and a social worker arrived to ask me questions. They led me away from the others to an empty area where we could talk. I had spent years protecting Lucinda, lying to teachers about my injuries and living conditions, but as I remembered Kevin's bruised and battered body on the stretcher, I let it all flow out of me. Tears I thought had dried up years ago fell from my eyes, hot and fast as I told them everything, the abuse, poor living conditions, unsavory people she had exposed us to, and all the people she had scammed over the years. They both took notes as I talked and allowed me time to compose myself as I sobbed through the tougher parts. I explained my fear of the system and being separated from Kevin. I told them about my "someday soon" plan and how I was afraid Kevin would die and I would never get to prove to him that someday soon did exist. They were both kind and reassured me none of it was my fault as I sobbed silently.

"If I would have reported her, Kevin wouldn't be hanging on for his life," I said brokenly.

"Katelyn, your mom has a sickness and that sickness is to blame for this, not you," the social worker said, giving me a sideways hug.

I felt drained from all the crying after talking with them and walked back to Max and his parents feeling lethargic. Karen seemed to sense my needs and led me to the far end of the ICU waiting room where a small loveseat sat. She pulled me down to sit with her and rested an arm around me, letting me lean against her. Max dragged a chair over silently and held my hand as I watched the slow-moving hands make their way around the clock on the wall near the door. Everyone remained silent while we waited, and I appreciated their presence. For so many years, it had seemed like it was just Kevin and me facing the world alone, so having them there made me feel loved.

Seven hours into our silent vigil, a tired looking surgeon entered the room. My supportive group huddled around me as he approached.

"Is he dead?" I asked, taking in his solemn expression.

"No, he's one lucky boy. He pulled through the surgery."

"He did?" I asked, not daring to believe him.

He nodded, smiling slightly. "The next twenty-four hours will be critical, and his body will need time to recover..." his words cutoff as I threw myself in his arms.

"Thank you so much," I said as tears of happiness rolled down my cheeks.

"It will be a long tough recovery," he cautioned, patting my back awkwardly. "And physical therapy will be a must."

"That's okay, we're not going anywhere," Max's dad said, reaching forward to shake the surgeon's hand too as he peppered him with questions about Kevin's injuries.

I tuned out their mumbo jumbo words and turned to Max who was grinning at me broadly as he pulled me into his arms. He led me to the other side of the room, away from the others.

"You okay?" he asked, pulling back slightly to gaze into my eyes.

"I'm getting there. I've never been so scared in my whole life."

"Neither have I," he admitted. "I was afraid you'd hate me for what we did tonight," he added, looking down at the ground, obviously feeling immense guilt.

"Oh," I said, thinking about it for the first time. "I guess I never really thought about that. Lucinda has always been a ticking time bomb and I've tried my hardest to limit her alone time with Kevin, but I just always thought if I took the brunt of her anger she would leave him alone. Tonight proved his safety was an illusion. If she wouldn't have lashed out tonight it would have happened down the road. I've taken the blame for so much over the years that this time I'm leaving the blame with her," I said.

Max pulled me back into his arms and placed his lips gently on mine.

"You know, I'm never letting you go now," he whispered against my lips.

"That's all I ask," I said as his lips claimed mine.

Epilogue

The days surrounding Kevin's recovery were a mixture of the happiest and worst days I had ever had. On his second day of his recovery, they discovered his brain was bleeding and they had to go in and repair the damage. They placed him in a drug-induced coma while the swelling in his brain went down.

Max's parents and the Graves's were lifesavers as they sat with me, offering support and comfort. Susan, the same social worker that had talked with me in the hospital that first night, came to visit every day and updated us on the red tape she was busily cutting through to get Maxwell and Karen approved as foster parents for Kevin and the Graves's for me. I had no idea that Max's parents wanted to foster us until his uncle showed up to the hospital that first night. We decided as a group that it would be easier if I stayed with the Graves's temporarily through the rest of the school year and the summer, since it would be awkward with Max and I dating. Max and I choose not to fill them in that we planned to live together the following year when we started college. I found it ironic that for years I had feared the system that I was convinced was against us, only to realize that they were actually on our side all along. After years of thinking we were alone, we were suddenly surrounded by people who all wanted us.

Lucinda made it easier when she signed away her parental rights as she awaited her sentencing. I wasn't sure why she finally decided to do something that was best for us, nor did I have plans to ever ask her. I had overlooked so much over the years that I could no longer find the strength to forgive her.

Max stayed with me the entire time I was at the hospital with Kevin, only leaving long enough to get us food and a change of clothing. Karen reassured me they had already moved our belongings and that Lucinda's stuff had been put in a storage unit to be dealt with later down the road.

One week after Kevin's brain had stopped bleeding they took him off the coma-induced medicine and told us it could be several hours before he came around and that he would be groggy when he woke.

Max and I sat on either side of him, anxiously waiting for him to wake. I was just beginning to doze off when I felt his hand move slightly in mine. I lifted my head off the bedrail and watched as his eyes slowly fluttered open.

"Hey, punk. You've been sleeping for a while," I said as tears fell down my cheeks.

"You're crying," he said.

I nodded. "You've been one sick little boy, and I've been very worried," I said, explaining my tears.

"Where am I?" he asked groggily.

"The hospital, pal. You've been here a while," I said, smiling with relief.

"What day is it?" he asked, looking at me a little more clearly.

"It's someday soon," I said through my tears as I looked at Kevin who smiled at me.

Other works **by Tiffany King**

Available on Amazon for the Kindle
And paperback

Meant to Be

(The Saving Angels book 1)

Forgotten Souls

(The Saving Angels book 2)

The Ascended

(The Saving Angels book 3)

CPSIA information can be obtained at www.ICGtesting.com
Printed in the USA
LVOW05s0320170314

377685LV00013B/288/P